Our Last CRUSADE OR THE RISE OF A New World

Secret File

2

KEI SAZANE

Illustration by

Ao Nekonabe

Our Last CRUSADE OR THE RISE OF A New World

Secret File 2

KEI SAZANE

Translation by Jan Cash
Cover art by Ao Nekonabe

KIMI TO BOKU NO SAIGO NO SENJO, ARUIWA SEKAI GA HAJIMARU SEISEN Secret File Vol. 2

First published in Japan in 2020 by KADOKAWA CORPORATION, Tokyo.
English translation rights arranged with KADOKAWA CORPORATION, Tokyo, through TUTTLE-MORI AGENCY, INC., Tokyo.

Yen On
150 West 30th Street, 19th Floor
New York, NY 10001

Visit us at yenpress.com
facebook.com/yenpress
twitter.com/yenpress
yenpress.tumblr.com
instagram.com/yenpress

First Yen On Edition: April 2024
Edited by Yen On Editorial: Maya Deutsch
Designed by Yen Press Design: Liz Parlett

Yen On is an imprint of Yen Press, LLC.
The Yen On name and logo are trademarks of Yen Press, LLC.

Library of Congress Cataloging-in-Publication Data
Names: Sazane, Kei, author. | Nekonabe, Ao, illustrator. | Cash, Jan Mitsuko, translator.
Title: Our last crusade or the rise of a new world: secret file / Kei Sazane ; illustration by Ao Nekonabe ; translation by Jan Cash.
Other titles: Kimi to boku no saigo no senjo, aruiwa sekai ga hajimaru seisen secret file (Light novel). English
Description: First Yen On edition. | New York, NY : Yen On, 2023-
Identifiers: LCCN 2023015916 | ISBN 9781975344290 (v. 1 ; trade paperback) | ISBN 9781975344313 (v. 2 ; trade paperback) | ISBN 9781975372514 (v. 3 ; trade paperback)
Subjects: CYAC: Fantasy. | Knights and knighthood—Fiction. | Krincesses—Fiction. | LCGFT: Fantasy fiction. | Short stories. | Light novels.
Classification: LCC PZ7.1.S297 Ov 2023 | DDC [Fic]—dc23

LC record available at https://lccn.loc.gov/2023015916

ISBNs: 978-1-9753-4431-3 (paperback)
978-1-9753-4432-0 (ebook)

10 9 8 7 6 5 4 3 2 1

LSC-C

Printed in the United States of America

Our Last CRUSADE OR THE RISE OF A New World

Secret File

So Se lu, Ee yum solin.
It parts.

Ee yum arsia Eeo-Ye-ckt kamyu bis xin peqqy.
You will hurt each other without remembering this time.

Lu Ee nec xedelis. Miqs, lu Ee tis-dia lan Zill qelno.
You don't need to turn back. Right now, just keep walking toward the future.

Utopia Powered by Machines

THE HEAVENLY EMPIRE

Iska

Member of Unit 907—Special Defense for Humankind, Third Division. Used to be the youngest soldier who ever reached the highest rank in the military, the Saint Disciples. Stripped of his title for helping a witch break out of prison. Wields a black astral sword to intercept astral power and its white counterpart to reproduce the last attack obstructed by its pair. An honest swordsman fighting for peace.

Mismis Klass

The commander of Unit 907. Baby-faced and often mistaken for a child, but actually a legal adult. Klutzy but responsible. Trusts her subordinates. Became a witch after plunging into a vortex.

Jhin Syulargun

The sniper of Unit 907. Prides himself on his deadly aim. Can't seem to shake off Iska, since they trained under the same mentor. Cool and sarcastic, though he has a soft spot for his buddies.

Nene Alkastone

Chief mechanic of Unit 907. Weapon-making genius. Mastered operation of a satellite that releases armor-piercing shots from a high altitude. Thinks of Iska as her older brother. Wide-eyed and loveable.

Risya In Empire

Saint Disciple of the fifth seat. Genius-of-all-trades. A beautiful woman often seen in a suit and glasses with dark green frames. Likes Mismis, her former classmate.

Nameless

The Saint Disciple of the eighth seat. He wears a full-body optical camouflage suit and speaks in an electronic voice. He originated from the assassin unit and boasts superior physical abilities.

Paradise of Witches

THE NEBULIS SOVEREIGNTY

Aliceliese Lou Nebulis IX

Second-born princess of Nebulis. Leading candidate for the next queen. Strongest astral mage, who attacks with ice. Feared by the Empire as the Ice Calamity Witch. Hates all the backstabbing happening in the Sovereignty. Enraptured by fair fights against Iska, an enemy swordsman she met on the battlefield.

Rin Vispose

Alice's attendant. An astral mage controlling earth. Maid uniform conceals weapons for assassination. Skilled at deadly espionage. Hard to read her expressions, but has an inferiority complex about her chest.

Mirabella Lou Nebulis VIII

The queen. Mother to Alice and her two sisters. A veteran who has been in charge of multiple battles. Seems to have history with Salinger, the transcendental sorcerer...

Elletear Lou Nebulis IX

Eldest princess of Nebulis. Focused on traveling abroad. Often absent from the palace.

Secret File

Our Last CRUSADE OR THE RISE OF A New World
Secret File

CONTENTS

File 01

Our Last Crusade or the Artist of Fire

Our Last CRUSADE OR THE RISE OF A New World
Secret File

CONFIDENTIAL

1

"We've blown our budget?!"

The Imperial capital, Yunmelngen.

In the metropolis of the largest military power in the world, Commander Mismis wailed, "What?! How did this happen, Iska?!"

"Shh. This'll be a disaster if a commanding officer overhears us." Iska held his finger to his lips in an attempt to quiet the commander down.

They were in an Imperial forces conference room, so one of their superiors could walk right down the hall at any moment.

"B-but how did this happen?!" Commander Mismis placed her head in her hands. Despite her childish behavior, petite appearance, and baby face, she was a full-grown twenty-two-year-old. "Iska, I just need to ask again. Are you sure that our unit blew the budget? You don't happen to mean *your* spending money?"

"Why would I blow through *my* money? I meant the *907's* annual budget."

"The one that HQ gives us each year as a lump sum?"

"That's it. The funds we use for procuring bullets for training, maintaining our guns, purchasing other equipment, and receiving medical checkups when we get injured. We blew through it all."

"Isn't that money super important?!"

That was exactly why he'd reported it to her.

Iska let out a sigh and pointed at a pile of documents on the desk.

"Well, just take a look at all these," Iska said. "We have a mountain of claim receipts."

"Since when?!" Mismis gingerly picked up one sheet from the gigantic pile. Then she stared at it so intensely, Iska thought she might bore holes right through the paper.

"What's this?" Mismis had no memory of submitting the claim in her hand. "Did you ask for this, Iska?"

"It wasn't me," Iska replied.

"Hey, do any of you know where this Derrick-made GAX22 new Gatling gun came from? I don't remember ever ordering this…"

"That's mine," Jhin, the silver-haired sniper, said. He was leaning back in his seat in a corner of the room. "It should come in next week. And we paid for it in one lump sum. You ordered it, boss."

"Jhin! This cost three months of our entire budget!"

"A soldier needs weapons." Jhin was flipping through the pages of a firearms catalog. He was considered a first-class sniper, and he made it a habit of checking out the latest guns available. "We're always trying to scrimp and save, so we can afford to splurge every once in a while."

"B-but I have more to say!" Mismis held an even more extravagant expense request in her hand. "What about this mono-channel wireless system Ebolba-made PQ9 tank? This is yours, too, isn't it, Jhin?!"

"Nope, I didn't order it."

"Huh? Then who did?" Mismis looked around the room. "Iska, you didn't..."

"Don't look at me," Iska said.

"But if it wasn't you or Jhin, then...then that means..."

"Uh-huh, yup! That's mine!" In another section of the room, a red-headed girl named Nene vigorously lifted her arm up as she trained with weights.

"Nene, this costs half our annual budget!"

"Aw, but...it's the super-popular new model, so there was only one left."

"Ugh... How could you all splurge on this stuff...?" Commander Mismis let out a small sigh.

Just then, Iska happened to look at the receipt at the very bottom of the pile. It appeared as though someone had tucked it away, so it would be out of sight.

"What's this one?" he asked.

"Ah! No, you can't, Iska!"

"'Full barbecue course for a meeting'? Huh? I don't remember any of us having a meeting at this place. Commander Mismis, do you know anything about this?"

"Urk!" She flinched.

Jhin, who had approached from the side, pulled out another receipt from a second barbecue restaurant.

"Hey, this one's from yesterday. What's going on, boss?"

"Oh. Um... It's not what it looks like..."

"Were you going around using our unit budget on barbecue places?"

"I—I was just...um...hungry and..."

"So you were?"

"I'm sorry!"

They'd caught the real culprit.

Jhin and Nene's expenditures had drained the budget close to depletion, but Mismis's daily barbecue binge had dealt the final blow.

"Everyone, listen! Nothing good will come from self-reflection! What's done is done. So we should look ahead and start saving up to make up our budget!" Mismis said.

"No, I think this *does* call for some self-reflection."

"I have a great idea!" Mismis ignored Jhin and plowed ahead, pulling out a part-time work agency magazine. "Ta-dah! We just need to get jobs!"

It just so happened that the Imperial forces allowed moonlighting. In fact, headquarters highly encouraged their soldiers to contribute to the rest of society.

"We could help people move heavy luggage or work as lifeguards at a pool or the beach. Or even teach people how to pitch tents for camp. There's tons of stuff we could do."

"Those won't net us enough cash." Jhin peered at the magazine. "We couldn't even pay back your barbecue bills with jobs like those, boss. Iska, have you found anything promising?"

"The best one is, uhhh...'Daiban Atelier assistant recruitment campaign.' I think that pays the highest."

In other words, they would be helping out at an artist's workshop. Famous artisans usually had apprentices, so it seemed unusual that this studio was requesting part-time assistance.

"Why not?! This is it, Iska!" Mismis excitedly said. "It pays the highest, after all!"

"But we'd be helping an *artist*. Are you sure amateurs like us should apply…?"

"It'll be fine. Besides, beggars can't be choosers. We need to save up enough to pay off these expenses!"

"I think we should discuss how much of our budget you spent on barbecue, boss…"

"So make sure your days off are free for work, everyone!" the commander declared, clutching the magazine.

2

The Imperial capital, Second Sector.

Their destination was at the edge of a large area where the residential and business districts met.

"Is this the Daiban Atelier?"

"Why is it a gigantic museum? It's like a golf course!"

The grounds of the studio were so vast that the building on the other side was blurry. When they spotted the atelier, which was integrated with a museum, Jhin and Commander Mismis both stopped in their tracks.

On the other hand…

Iska didn't even bother to hide his surprise when faced with the fantastical ambience oozing from the art museum.

"Th-this is—" he stuttered.

"Iska?"

"How did I not notice? This is the atelier of *that* Daiban, the living national treasure!"

Appreciating the arts was one of Iska's hobbies. It didn't seem like a pastime one of the most distinguished swordsmen in the

Empire would engage in, but he was a fine arts fiend and would often travel to faraway neutral cities for museum visits.

Iska couldn't stop the shudders that racked his body.

"Commander, a world-renowned artist works here!"

"What? Really?"

"The human treasure, Daiban! They call him the Artist of Fire!"

The artist worked in all forms of art from ceramics to calligraphy, poetry, sculpture, painting, music, and even gourmet food—and he always pushed each medium to its fullest potential. That was Daiban. His name was known worldwide, and he had die-hard fans in nations all over the world.

"Some people think that as long as he lives in the Imperial capital, the Sovereignty won't launch an all-out war. He's famous enough for rumors like that to exist about him."

"The Sovereignty?!"

"Yes. If anything were to happen to him, it would be a huge loss to the world."

Was he really such a formidable man that he could sway the Sovereignty, which saw the world in black and white when it came to the Empire?

It sounded too good to be true.

"Actually, I've heard of him, too," Jhin murmured. "Supposedly there's an old man with more authority than a king living in the Imperial capital. You don't mean that—"

"Exactly!" A large man appeared in the entrance and immediately answered the sniper's question. "I'm his top apprentice, Gorie. Welcome to Master Daiban's atelier!"

The man was about the height of three Mismises stacked from head to toe. Though his features were friendly, he looked like a pro wrestler from the neck down, which gave him a mismatched look.

"Are you the part-timers from the military? Three in total, then?"

"Y-yes! I'm Commander Mismis. This is Iska, and that's Jhin."

Nene was spending her day off doing military training exercises.

"I'll introduce you to the master straightaway. Follow me!" Gorie led them into the workshop behind the museum.

"Th-this artist might be a lot more famous than I thought. Say, Jhin, are you sure we're gonna be okay?"

"I don't know the first thing about art," Jhin answered.

"What about you, Iska?!"

"I'm not very confident I can do this, either…," Iska said, mirroring everyone's sentiments. He was just an art enthusiast. He didn't know anything about making it. He couldn't even imagine what they'd be asked to do.

"Master! Master!" Gorie knocked on a door labeled PRODUCTION ROOM.

"The part-timers from the Imperial forces are here. We're coming in!"

He barged in without waiting for a response.

And there they saw…

"Nuaaaagh!"

A growling elderly man.

This was Daiban, the living treasure. He sported a full white beard and was large enough to rival the size of his apprentice. His eyes glinted with the intensity of a warrior.

"Hrmm…This won't work!"

He hadn't noticed Iska and the others yet. Even his top apprentice hadn't seemed to have gotten through to him, as he hadn't taken his eyes off his current work, a painting.

"Sir, the part-timers—"

"I can't believe it… How could I create such an uninspired painting?!"

Daiban stood up. As the master artist picked up a bright red statue placed along a wall filled with many other similar sculptures, Gorie cried out, "Blast! Everybody, get down on the ground!"

"What?"

"Master Daiban is a perfectionist. He can't bear to leave any mistakes in this world, so he makes sure to wipe them from existence—with explosives!"

They all instantly ducked. Being Imperial forces members, Iska's team had no trouble quickly getting out of the way of explosives.

"Begone, you bungled job!"

Daiban threw the statue at the painting. Then it exploded—and spectacularly at that. There was a roar accompanied by a rush of fire as the painting burst into flames.

Daiban was known as the Artist of Fire.

Though he was a living treasure, he was also infamous in the Imperial capital for being dangerous.

"*Haah...haah...* This is my true masterpiece, the *Statue of Despair*! This way, my blunders can at least bring beauty to this world as they're blown to smithereens."

"You almost blew us to smithereens, too, you know!"

"Hm?" The man finally turned around. It seemed he really hadn't noticed anyone was there until Mismis shouted at him.

"Wh-what was that explosion?!"

"Oho, a young lady. Are you interested in my masterpiece, the *Statue of Despair*?"

"Not even a little bit!"

His so-called masterpiece was a method of blowing up his rejected works.

After watching the statue explode with the slightest impact, Iska and the others were filled with the urge to back away until they noticed another dozen more *Statues of Despair* lining the wall. They had enough military training to know what that involved.

"Well, sir, if you would," Goric said, offering the part-timers up.

"Mm-hmm. I am the nation's living treasure Daiban!"

The artist gave them a hearty nod and pointed directly at Mismis, who was in front of him.

"You, young lady—tell me what art is!"

"What? I don't know how to answer if you put me on the spot! I'm just a soldier. This is way out of my depth..."

"Then I'll teach you!" The brawny man looked at Mismis, Iska, and Jhin, then raised a fist in the air. "Art is a battle with the universe within you! You build up your spirit and your creativity until you create a new universe. You get my drift?"

"I think this old man would be better off committed." Jhin muttered an off-color comment.

But Daiban himself had said everything he wanted and had already turned around.

"Whew... Doesn't matter when—teaching the youth always gets me fired up."

"You haven't taught us anything, though," Jhin objected.

"Now, you all go out and find your own new universes and create art for the new era."

"Like I just said—"

"Gor!" Daiban summoned his apprentice. He was ignoring Jhin, of course. "I'm a busy man. Gor, you watch them."

"I'll take over, then. All right, part-timers, to the courtyard! Allow me to introduce you to all the art the master has made."

Courtyard of the workshop.

The lush green lawn was almost like a golf course. The courtyard had been made to serve as an outdoor exhibition hall.

"Wow! There's a lot of people!"

"We get plenty of tourists from overseas. Daiban is famous all over the world, after all."

Iska and company followed Gorie to an incomplete area of the courtyard that was not yet open to the public.

"You're all lucky. We have an established custom of showing part-timers a generous sample of the master's greatest works. All pieces are famous."

"What? Really?"

"Of course. We start here!" Gorie pointed at a sculpture.

Iska thought it looked a little like a three-legged cephalopod.

...Is that an octopus? Or maybe a jellyfish?

...No, wait, it's definitely a mollusk.

He hadn't heard of a three-legged mollusk before, though. He considered outright asking what it was. But he also knew that his question could be interpreted as a slight to the artist.

"Huh? What's this supposed to be? It looks like something a kid made."

"Commander, did you really just say that?!"

Gorie didn't seem to take offense at all.

"Ha-ha, the master is famous for being incredibly creative with his art. Now, let me teach you all about it. This is an early representative of Daiban's work—*Dogfight*. Look at that wonderful energy."

"Is this jellyfish supposed to be a...dog?"

"Yes. And the way it squishes around like that is how he expresses its vigor. It's brimming with the power and energy of dogs in a scuffle."

It really wasn't.

It just looked too much like a jellyfish for Unit 907 to see it as anything but. Iska, Mismis, and Jhin all battled the urge to voice their impressions as they exchanged glances.

"Hey, boss, don't you think a kid could come up with something better than this? Are you sure that old man is actually famous?"

"I-I've been wanting to ask that, too! Iska, you know a lot about art, don't you? What do you think of this?"

"Uh, um...I'm afraid I don't know enough about this style of art..."

"Hey, I'm going to just ask." Jhin wasn't one to feel daunted. "I have no clue how much this statue is worth. Could you explain that to me?"

"An excellent question!" Gorie nodded. "When art is too advanced for its time, the people don't understand it. Though progressive art attempts to break new ground, history shows that it can cause all kinds of problems and tragedies—"

"Okay, get to the point. Just tell me the value of this thing in terms of cold, hard cash."

"You'd be able to buy a whole Imperial military aircraft by selling one of these—one of the new aircrafts, even."

"What?!" Mismis yelled.

The broke members of Unit 907 had a huge case of sticker shock.

"You could get rich with this sculpture alone... Maybe I should become an artist, too," Mismis said.

"How ridiculous! Master was only able to produce this statue after doing years of research into beauty. You can't mimic this that easily."

"I think I *could*, though..." Mismis eyed the sculpture of what definitely looked like a three-tentacled jellyfish.

"Then is there a deeper reason why this statue of a dog looks like a jellyfish?"

"Of course, that was an aspect he deeply considered." Gorie was full of confidence. "The master once said this regarding the subject: 'I sneezed so hard that I broke off one of the legs.'"

"How did that involve any consideration?!"

"Allow me to show you his next masterpiece!" Gorie cut Mismis off and continued walking.

"Uh, wait!"

The next work was displayed on a marble pedestal.

"Even now, Daiban is still brimming with inspiration. This statue is part of his collection from this year—Work No. 7, the *Singing Fruit*, the first of its series. What do you think?"

This one was a hand grenade.

It was as though someone had taken a disabled bomb right off the production line and plopped it on a pedestal.

That was all it was.

"Iska, I—"

"Wait, Commander! You don't need to say everything that comes to mind… Besides, I agree with you."

He couldn't wrap his head around it. Iska could tell that the strange jellyfish-dog abstraction was a sculpture, at least. But this?

"Mr. Gorie, where's Master Daiban's piece?"

"It's right in front of your eyes."

"But all I see is a disabled grenade."

"Then I'll explain it to you!" Gorie whipped his finger out and pointed it at the explosive.

"This installation—in which the artist likens this cute, round grenade to a fruit that 'sings' through exploding—could not have been completed without Daiban's inventiveness, compositional skills, and genius grasp of poetics. It really showcases his *explosive* knack for art."

"Even I could just set a deactivated bomb on a pedestal," Jhin murmured.

Gorie's eyes glittered when he picked up Jhin's comment.

"Jhin, was it? I'm afraid that's a big misconception."

"What?"

"Take a look at that intact pin. This is a genuine article bought right from Imperial headquarters. It's still quite capable of detonating!"

"That's even worse! How could you expose an undetonated grenade to the elements like this?!"

Headquarters was also firmly against the illegal trafficking of weapons.

...Or they should have been, at least.

"Daiban has some secret fans at headquarters, you see. They're generous folks. They don't mind sneaking him one or two dozen grenades."

"What a ridiculous old man. Make sure he stores those safely!"

"They're in the Production Room we were in earlier."

"That's the most dangerous spot he could put them!"

The grenades were in the same room as the *Statues of Despair.* If even one of them accidentally ignited...

"I'm pretty sure handling undetonated grenades would fall under the hazardous material treatment laws. We better report this right aw—"

"All right, on to the next piece!"

"Hey!"

Ignoring Jhin, Gorie headed farther into the courtyard.

"We've only looked at Daiban's man-made art so far. Next, we'll see the vivid pieces he created while grappling with nature."

This one was another piece from that year, New Work No. 13, *Mother Nature.* That was what was written on a small label at the entrance of the museum.

It turned out to be a single desiccated leaf.

Iska and the others didn't want to believe it, but...

"This is the master's newest piece."

"I knew it!"

All three of them had the exact same reaction.

"This is just a single fallen leaf. But you can feel the distilled energy from Mother Nature emanating from it, can't you? The way he purposefully placed it on concrete to highlight its vivid green hue can only be described as magnificent."

"Uh, that's just a dry leaf..."

"And it's not even green. It's brown..."

"And that thing's definitely lost whatever energy from Mother Nature it had when it dried up..."

"Allow me to continue my explanation!" Gorie was hearing none of the very valid points that Iska and his unit were making. "We auctioned off the right to be the first person to view this piece to four hundred aristocrats from all over the world."

"Four hundred?!"

"How much spare time do these aristocrats even have?!"

"They had a tough fight for five hours, and in the end, the auction finished at a sum that was easily on the same level as the Imperial forces' total budget."

"I don't get it! It just doesn't make sense!" Commander Mismis's eyes were completely out of focus. "This little leaf is just...ah!"

As Mismis pointed at the leaf, it floated off on the wind. Then it flew beyond the garden and disappeared from sight.

"Did his newest work just disappear on us?!"

"Wh-what do we do now?!"

"Please calm down, everyone. That's exactly what I'm here for." Gorie confidently raised his hand.

Then he bent down and picked up a leaf in the courtyard, painstakingly placing it in the same spot the earlier leaf had been in.

"......Whew." He was sweating bullets, and his expression was grim, as though he had just fought in a battle that would decide the very fate of the world. "I just barely managed to fix it."

"How?!"

"You didn't manage to fix anything!"

"And this one's a green leaf instead of a dry one now!"

When it comes to art, it seems that anything goes. Even Unit 907's protests couldn't shake Gorie's overpowering confidence.

"Lastly, I'll show you the piece Master Daiban is proudest of," he said.

This one was Masterpiece No. 9, *Lord.*

But wasn't it just a fuzzy dog? Or maybe a curled-up cat? Based on the name of the work, the sculpture had to be modeled off the supreme authority of the Empire, the Lord, but the piece in front of them definitely didn't look human.

"His Excellency was absolutely thrilled by this statue and appointed Master Daiban a national living treasure because of it."

"Uh-huh..."

"What even *is* art...?"

"I'm starting to worry about the state of our country."

Apparently, this sculpture was priceless. Supposedly, it was considered so sublime that the appraisers had been left in a state of dread after laying eyes on it.

"Once, a would-be thief broke in, but when they saw this piece, their soul was purified. They were sobbing as they turned themselves in."

"That can't be true!"

"There's no way it would make them cry!"

"Now this is sounding like some weird cult thing."

The three of them looked at each other. They weren't even trying to hide the fact that they were exchanging bewildered glances in front of Daiban's apprentice.

"What do we do, boss? Do you think we can actually work at a place like this? I don't think I could understand the old guy's art even if I wanted to. There's no way I can help him."

"Uh… I'm not confident I could work here, either. Iska, I'm leaving it in your hands!"

"B-but I can't, either!"

Even Iska, who loved art, couldn't make heads or tails of Daiban's oeuvres. Jhin and Mismis had already given up trying to understand entirely.

"All right, I think it's about time to get you started on the actual work."

"Grk?!"

"Now, come with me."

Ignoring the fact that he'd frightened all three of the part-timers, Gorie energetically pointed ahead.

Daiban Atelier.

Music Room.

"This is the room Master Daiban shuts himself into when he's composing music."

It was filled with classical musical instruments, such as a piano, a violin, and a trumpet. There were even rows of indigenous instruments from various countries.

"Wow! This place is huge! It might even be as big as the forces' large conference room."

"It's pretty messy, though."

When the commander and Jhin looked in, they saw hundreds of sheets of handwritten musical scores strewn all over the floor. Stacks of scores were also piled up on the desk. Some had even been pinned to the walls and ceiling, meaning there were probably some thousands of sheets of music in all.

Just then, Iska noticed something.

"Oh. Is this an opera?"

There were stage directions written in the margins of some scores. Opera was a fusion of theater and choir. The art form was so popular that some called it the queen of arts. Iska had even traveled to the opera house in a neutral city in the past to watch a performance.

"Oh, I know what those are!" Mismis said, suddenly seeming motivated. She started to pick up the sheets of music strewn on the ground. "Wow. That's a huge chorus, plus the solo and accompaniment seem fancy—"

"Exactly!" Gorie suddenly held up a stack of sheet music. "This is unmistakably an opera. And it's no ordinary opera, either. These thousands of sheets of music are meant for a single musical piece!"

"What?!"

"Th-that's something..."

How many hundreds of people were supposed to be in this production? They'd have to spend dozens of hours onstage, too.

"This is Master Daiban's once-in-a-lifetime grand chorus. It's called *Our Last Crusade or the Rise of a New World Love Sonata*!"

"Wow!"

"Based on that name, it's got to be a great work..."

"Compared to the sculptures from earlier, this is way better," agreed Jhin, who was definitely no purveyor of fine art.

An opera that needed that much sheet music had to be good.

"I'm sure you can feel all the passion imbued within the handwritten scores! It contains a ballad that offers a new world to the new generation, and a requiem that leads grieving souls suffering from heartbreak to solace!"

"W-well, that's something..."

"I—I think even I get that it's a really big deal?" Mismis said.

"It has spirit, at the very least."

"Alas, the project is so big that it's remained unfinished since it was commissioned thirty years ago."

""""Then it's doomed!"""" Unit 907 cried out in a chorus of their own. Their voices echoed throughout the music room.

Daiban had started this project three decades ago. The commissioner must have been incredibly patient. They had to wonder how the person was feeling as they waited for the artist to finish.

"Now, let's keep going. So about the opera, *Our Last Crusade or the Rise of a New World Love Sonata*—which I'll call *Last Love* for short..."

"...Oh. That suddenly makes it feel more accessible."

"Sure, okay...," Jhin said.

"It sounds pretty cute. I like it," Mismis added.

"This right here makes up all the sheet music that Master Daiban rejected. Basically, I'd like to ask you to clean this up."

He was referring to the pages strewn about on the desk and floor.

Upon closer inspection, they saw that some of the sheets had been haphazardly scribbled over, while others had been torn up in a fit of artistic frenzy.

"Normally, Master Daiban would just throw a *Statue of Despair* at these pages and burn them like any other botched work, but there are some important scores in here, too. Instead, we'd like you to tear them into tiny pieces using a shredder."

"Okay! That seems like something we could do." Commander Mismis felt relieved as she enthusiastically raised her hand. "We'll do our very best!"

"I'm counting on you. Now, I'm going to go help the master. I'll be back in an hour."

They got to work on their new assignment.

It turned out that shredding paper was a lot more work than Iska and the others had expected. They were cleaning up a mess that was thirty years in the making, after all. And there were several thousand sheets to deal with. Some of the pages of the score had been relegated to the corners of the room and were covered in dust.

"*Cough*... *Cough*... Hey, Iska," Mismis said. "The dust is really bad over here."

"My sheets have mold growing all over them," Iska replied. "I'm glad I brought gloves just in case."

He was also wearing a mask.

As Iska and Mismis systematically shredded the paper, Jhin took the scraps and packed them into plastic bags.

However...

Things spiraled out of control from there.

"Urgh. The shredder is jammed?! What's going on? There's oil paint stuck to these!"

"Oww! Someone dropped the blade of a chisel over here!"

The shredder kept breaking down on them. And even though they were in the music room, there were blades from sculpting tools mixed in with the sheet music.

"Iska, the shredder isn't working..."

"It's probably overheated. We're trying to run it at full capacity when it probably hasn't been used in years. Commander, I see some scissors over there—how about we cut them by hand?"

They switched over to shredding the sheet music the old-fashioned way. But there were still mountains of paper left.

"Huh? Commander Mismis, that particular score looks

important since it's held together by a clip. Are you sure you should be cutting it?"

"It's all right, no worries." Commander Mismis hummed as she trimmed away the score with her scissors. "This was also on the ground. Daiban would put the important music on his desk, of course. So this has to be one of the pieces he wants to get rid of."

"Got it."

An hour passed...

"So how's it going?" Gorie came back, sounding as upbeat as ever. "Oh, the shredder stopped working, so I see you've switched to manual labor. Sorry about that."

"It's all right. We just finished!" Commander Mismis said.

They'd shredded everything, stuffed all the paper into bags, and even swept away the dust. The music room looked brand-new.

"Splendid! The Imperial forces have always had skilled members. I'm sure the master will also...huh?"

Gorie looked around the room.

"What's wrong, Mr. Gorie?"

"Huh? I'm pretty sure there was a score held together by a clip on the desk. Maybe it fell on the floor?"

"They were clipped together?"

"It's the completed eighth movement, so we tried to keep it separated from the rest."

The entire unit fell silent.

Jhin and Iska stared at the scissors in Commander Mismis's hand.

"Commander..."

"C'mon..."

"S-so, um..."

Commander Mismis gulped, sweating buckets. Then she stuck out her finger.

"I think it might be in there…"

She pointed at the plastic bags. The musical scores were in there, shredded into an unrecognizable form.

"What?!"

"I-I'm sorry, Mr. Gorie!"

"I—I mean… Everyone makes mistakes. We only lost a part of it, and that's nothing compared to the whole thing." Even Gorie looked like he was panicking. "Let's apologize to the master. The best thing to do is to be honest."

"D-do you think he'll forgive us?"

"…"

"Why aren't you saying anything?!"

"I-it'll be fine… Master Daiban is very strict on himself and others, but he has the capacity to forgive honest mistakes."

As worry came to Commander Mismis's face, Gorie gave her a gentle pat on the shoulder.

"I think he'll forgive you after he carves a pattern into your back with a chisel."

"No thank you!"

Daiban Atelier.

Production Room.

When Iska peeked into the room, he saw the artist Daiban at its center.

"Ngaaaah?!"

But there was something off about him. He was standing in front of a statue of a young woman and groaning as though he was grappling with something.

"Wrong… This isn't what I imagine when I think of a young lady!"

"That's the master's next work," Gorie sneakily informed them from behind the door.

Its title was *Chrysalis and Butterfly*. He was attempting to depict the anguish of a girl on the cusp of womanhood as her body takes on its adult form. But if he emphasized her womanliness, the statue would lose some of its girlish innocence. On the other hand, when he focused on emphasizing a girl's childlike nature, the statue no longer seemed mature.

"Master? Master Daiban?"

"Uraaaaaaah!"

"Master!"

"Gwaaaaah!"

It was no use. He was completely oblivious to their presence.

Even though the four of them were standing right behind him.

"This won't do. I only have a month to complete it for the summer grand exhibition! But I haven't found the perfect girl yet!"

Daiban started to run his hands through his hair. Just then, he turned around.

"Oh? What is it, Gor? And what are you all here for?"

"Actually, sir—"

"Hm? You!" Daiban pushed aside his apprentice and leaned forward. He stared at Commander Mismis without blinking as she gaped back at him.

"What? You mean me?" she asked.

"It's you!"

"Eep?!"

Mismis was terrified as he grabbed her shoulders, but the old man was so engrossed in whatever he'd found that he didn't notice.

"You're my ideal young lady!"

"Excuse me?!"

Mismis had an innocent face and the height of a child, but she was a twenty-two-year-old. And as an adult woman, she was very well-developed at the bust and hips—even more so than the typical person. She perfectly embodied the duality of "girl" and "woman" that Daiban was looking for.

"You're brimming with naughtiness!"

"But I'm not naughty! I'm innocent!" Mismis turned red and yelled, but Daiban, the living treasure, was already raising his voice.

"Take off your clothes!"

"Whaaat?!"

"Hold up, old man." Jhin stopped Daiban from behind before the artist could corner Mismis. "That's not part of the job. If you want her to model, you'll have to compensate us fairly."

"Oh?"

"But you haven't asked whether I would model, Jhin!"

"Calm down, boss. Would you rather he carve a design into your back? Think about which is better."

"I don't wanna do either!"

But the deal was struck.

Mismis was formally selected as Daiban's model. In exchange, he declared Unit 907 even for destroying part of *Last Love*.

However...

Even though Daiban requested that Mismis model in the buff, she was adamant in turning him down. Instead, they settled on having her pose in her underwear.

"Wow, Jhin. You really saved us there."

"That was an easy bargain to make."

"Iska! Jhin! Why are you two just drinking tea and abandoning me, your own commander?!"

Mismis was on the sofa in the Production Room, sprawled

out in her underwear. Her whole face was red, and her shoulders quivered.

"Well, we got into this mess because *you* spent our budget on barbecue."

"Urgh!"

She went silent at Iska's rebuttal.

It looked like she had resigned herself to her fate. The petite, baby-faced commander let out a huge sigh.

"Th-this is art. I'm doing art… I-it's not embarrassing at all…"

"This is it! This was the ideal body of a young lady that I was searching for! My creative juices are overflowing!" Daiban shouted in delight.

He was sketching intensely on canvas to get Mismis's form down before he started sculpting.

However…

Iska and Jhin found his drawing just as inscrutable as his earlier works.

"Oh. The boss has got five eyes in this."

"Is that a thorn poking out between her breasts? Maybe they're antennae?"

"I haven't got any of those!"

As the drawing solidified, it turned into something from a nightmare—the kind of stuff that would make little kids cry.

…Or it seemed like it should have.

"Oh, shoot!"

"What's wrong, Master?"

Daiban stopped sketching. Deep wrinkles lined his forehead as he compared Mismis to her drawing over and over again.

"Hmm… Something's not quite right. There's no wisdom in her."

"You've got that right, old man. Looks like you actually do have good judgment."

"Whose side are you on, Jhin?!"

"It feels like... No, it's too soon. I shouldn't settle so early into the process..."

Daiban staggered away, leaving the Production Room with the help of his apprentice.

"Gor, I'm going to meditate and rest for a while."

"Yes, sir. As for you all..." Gorie gestured around the messy room. "Could you clean here, too?"

The place was filled with the remnants of failed paintings, torn sketches, and even scraps of fabric covered in pigments.

"As I've explained, the master has established that all works other than his finished pieces are to be wiped out of existence with fire. Please use this stove to burn them all up."

"A-all right!"

After waiting for Mismis to get dressed, the three of them got to work cleaning.

It was a lot easier than the shredder and the musical scores. All they had to do was stick everything in the stove and burn it away.

"Hey, Iska," Mismis said. "This stove sure is big."

"I think it's specially made for ceramics firing. Master Daiban is famous for those, too."

They could throw the human-size statues and canvases straight in.

"Boss, that huge thing against the wall looks like it's the largest piece."

"It's so big! I couldn't carry that on my own. Iska, Jhin, give me a hand."

It was a wooden carving about two yards in length. In any

case, it was gigantic, and they also had no idea what it was meant to represent.

Maybe it was some kind of animal?

There was a single tentacle coming out of the statue that left quite an impression.

"Jhin, do you think this is an animal?"

"How should I know? It's probably like that jellyfish-dog thing. I think he just accidentally added a tentacle when he didn't mean to."

"Oh, I guess you're right."

The three of them worked together to hurl the carving into the stove.

"Urgh… There's another one of these things."

"How many times does he have to make the same mistake before he's satisfied?"

They also threw the second one into the stove. With that, they'd cleaned out the biggest failed pieces of art. Now they just needed to get rid of the scraps of paper and discarded clay.

"Okay! Let's light it up!"

The flames in the stove flared.

Just then, Daiban and his apprentice came back.

"Oh, looks like you did a good job cleaning up. Yup, a clean slate means a fresh start. I'm sure the master will really be back at it soon."

"…Hm?"

"Master?"

"I have a question, you all." Daiban turned to Iska and company, pointing at a section of the room. "I had two giant sculptures right over there. Do you remember them?"

"Yeah, I do!" Mismis raised her hand heartily. "We found them while cleaning, so—"

"Ah, so you moved them," Daiban said.

"We burned them!" Mismis continued.

Crack. At that moment, they could practically hear Daiban and his apprentice's expressions freeze and fissure.

"......What did you just say?"

"Yeah, we made sure to burn them while we were cleaning. They were the biggest pieces, so it was such a hassle moving them. Right, Jhin?"

"Yeah, those cursed sculptures were real heavy. Right, Iska?"

"It was so hard getting them into the stove."

The three of them were still oblivious.

The world-renowned artist was quivering, and his apprentice was turning paler by the second.

"..."

"What's wrong, old man? Are you scared that the room's so clean now?"

The living treasure of the Empire faltered.

"Th-those were the works of my soul... A princess from a faraway country commissioned them... They were my magnum opuses...!"

"What?"

What had the man said? His magnum opuses?

"What? Wait, you don't mean...?"

"Surely you're joking, right, Master Daiban? They were so creepy..."

"They were huge, frightening, and they even had tentacles coming out of them."

The three of them were talking quickly.

"Those two pieces were called the *One-Winged Divine Birds.* I was planning to announce them as some of my greatest works..."

He staggered over to the raging stove. There, he stared at the bright red flames.

"Those weren't tentacles. They were wings."

"Those carvings were birds?"

"But they each only had one wing."

"Yes, that's just weird, old man. Birds and planes need two wings to fly."

Unit 907 tried to reason with him.

The artist only nodded silently.

"Yes, that's why they came as a pair. The two of them together formed a single whole. The idea was that they would use their pair of shared wings to fly."

"......"

"They would help each other aim for the skies. Yes, those pieces were meant to represent the human way of life. They were statues of birds, yes, but they were also supposed to show how humans are incomplete but strive to live anyway!"

Oh, this is bad. Iska, Jhin, and Mismis came to the same realization simultaneously.

Even though the sculptures had seemed cursed and looked nothing like birds to them before, they could now picture the idealized beauty the old man was trying to describe.

They couldn't make excuses now.

"And you...you..."

"W-wait, Master Daiban!"

They were too late. They couldn't think of anything to say before he shouted, "Open the curtains!"

Suddenly, Daiban produced chisels from out of nowhere. He thrust out their tips, which were sharp as knives.

"My soul's magnum opus has been stolen from me. This is the

name of my revenge as an artist—*Ceremony, the Beautiful Theater.* And now the curtains on the act rise!"

"This can't be happening?!"

"W-wait a second!"

"How were we supposed to know that was your magnum opus?"

Neither Iska nor Jhin nor Mismis had noticed that Gorie had already slipped away while no one was looking.

"And for the finale, I'm going to carve patterns into you all using my chisels!"

The old man leaped up.

He seemed to soar into the air, as though the spirits of the divine birds that had gone up in flames had taken possession of him.

"Get ready for what's coming!"

"Ahhhh?!"

"Oh no! This is even worse than what happened with the sheet music!"

"R-retreat!"

They started to run for it.

But this was Daiban's fortress. No matter where they ran at full speed, Daiban would be one step ahead of them, blocking their path.

"I'm not letting you escape!"

He ran after them with a chisel in each hand.

"I'll turn you all into living pieces of art!"

"No way!"

Unit 907 ran all over the workshop.

"Huh?"

"Does something smell like it's burning?"

"Is that the scent of gunpowder…?"

The three of them stopped running once they came back to the Production Room again.

The giant stove was blazing.

Even though it was supposed to be heat-resistant, the entire device was engulfed in flames.

"What's going on?!"

"Shoot! It's over capacity!" Iska felt anxious. "It's because we put in those two birds, or whatever they were. They were too big... and now the stove's going to explode, Commander!"

"So they *were* cursed in the end!"

However...

A certain artist barred their escape, a chisel in each hand.

"Ha-ha-ha-ha! I've finally cornered you!"

"He's here!"

"W-wait, Master Daiban! Behind you! Your Production Room is on fire!"

"Your whole workshop will burn down!"

"A fire? Hmph, I won't fall for your bluffs. You want me to turn around so you can run."

The whole room was ablaze. But Daiban laughed their warning off, not believing what was happening behind him.

"You think I'm scared of a little fire? Fools! That'll never work on me!"

The blood drained from Unit 907's faces.

Not because of Daiban. The flames had just reached the many, many *Statues of Despair* in the room, which were filled with gunpowder.

"Like I just said—"

"Old man, those statues are going to explode behind you."

"I don't wanna die!"

"Ridiculous!" Daiban laughed off their cries, flinging out both of his arms and staring up at the ceiling. "You think it'll burn down? Ha-ha. I'll tell you something. Just as the arts will last forever, so, too, will my workshop— Hm?"

The embers had started to land on his head. The Production Room had burned down, and the flames were starting to move into the hallway right behind Daiban.

"What's this?"

He looked up at the embers and finally turned around.

"A fire?!"

"We told you!"

"Didn't we just say that?!"

"It's too late! We can't extinguish it now!"

Three minutes passed.

As for the Daiban Atelier…

It let off a beautiful flash of light before it exploded to smithereens.

The next day.

In a room in the Nebulis Sovereignty, far, far away from the Empire.

"There was a giant explosion in the Imperial capital?" Alice said as she read a periodical.

She was a princess with brilliant golden hair and a lovely face, but the Empire feared her as the Ice Calamity Witch. Despite the tension between the Sovereignty and the Empire, she and Iska were secret rivals.

"And the explosion occurred at Daiban Atelier?! This is a huge deal!"

Daiban was the Artist of Fire.

The Empire was technically an enemy, but Alice was a fan of Daiban's work. When he had gone on a trip around the world once, she'd spent three days and nights chasing after him to commission a piece.

"I hope he's all right. I hope the sculpture is, too..."

The work she'd commissioned was called *One-Winged Divine Birds.*

I'd like beautiful birds.

That had been Alice's request for the two-sculpture piece. She had even gotten word that he was almost done with them.

"No, I must have faith in him!"

She stood up in her living room.

"I'm sure he and the sculptures are fine. Yes, what I need to do now is figure out where to put them."

The palace courtyard would probably be perfect. Then she could enjoy gazing at the sculptures with her vassals.

"...Oh. And with Iska, too!"

She wanted to send him a picture of them. She was sure he would be shocked to see them, considering he also appreciated the fine arts.

"Hee-hee. I hope you'll be surprised, Iska. Soon I'll be able to show you the legendary Master Daiban's work in person!"

As she took up a vitalizing spot by the window, Alice looked in the direction of the Imperial territory with full confidence.

Meanwhile, at the same time...

"It burned down..."

"That was a pretty big explosion..."

"We're covered in soot..."

Iska and the others were at the former site of Daiban Atelier. They all stared at the estate, which had been rendered to ash, in bewilderment.

On the other hand...

"Sir, you look refreshed."

"Oh, my top apprentice. Now that I think about it, this is a great opportunity. I'm going to construct the new workshop I've come up with!" said the Artist of Fire, Daiban.

Days later, the world was moved when he broke the news that he would be constructing the New Daiban Atelier, which would be the largest art workshop in the Imperial capital.

"Stop staring, you three! Help me clean, why don't you?"

"Y-yes, sir!"

To make it up to Daiban for burning his art, Unit 907 had volunteered to help clean up. Without pay, of course.

"Waaaah! But since we worked for free, our budget is just the same as before!"

"Well, the whole problem started with your barbecue bill, Commander."

"Guess our only option is to find a slightly better job next time," Jhin said.

And as for their next job...

It would also end in catastrophe, but that's a story for another time.

File 02

Our Last Crusade or the Spy Mission Training

Our Last CRUSADE OR THE RISE OF A New World

Secret File

CONFIDENTIAL

1

"There are traitorous spies among us!"

They were at an Imperial base. Commander Mismis had started off that day's meeting with that rather dramatic declaration.

"Or at least, HQ wants us to make that happen during training," she said. "Iska, what do you think we should do?"

"Isn't this kind of coming out of nowhere?" The Imperial swordsman tilted his head quizzically. "If you could start from the beginning..."

"You already know the story, Iska. Some Nebulis spies tried to invade the Imperial capital."

Two global superpowers were at war. The Heavenly Empire that Iska and his companions were part of had waged an ongoing, century-long campaign against the Nebulis Sovereignty, otherwise known as the Paradise of Witches. Since the conflict was currently at a standstill, they'd resorted to sending spies into each other's territories.

"Yeah, of course I heard about that. It happens every year. There were two or three suspicious people caught on the surveillance cameras in the capital."

"That's right. We think they're from the Nebulis Sovereignty's intelligence unit." Commander Mismis nodded.

Yes. Enemy spies had already invaded the Empire.

"The Empire is just too big. There are so many people within its territory that it's impossible to investigate every single person who comes in from overseas."

"We've got physical limitations..."

Since Iska was an Imperial soldier, the problem struck close to home.

Luckily, the Empire's most important secrets—its military intelligence—had yet to be breached. The Imperial forces' security had blocked all attempts at espionage.

"We can't let our guard down, Iska. We need to assume that a Nebulis spy might even target this base."

"Oh, so that's why..."

"Yeah, that's right. It's the theme of our training." Commander Mismis pointed to a map of the Empire on the wall. "I christen this the 'Betray the Imperial Forces Mission!' We'll become spies and infiltrate the Imperial base!"

"Well, that's a very...novel idea," Iska replied.

"I know, right?" Mismis said. "Jhin, Nene, did you catch all of that?"

"I got all of it. Sounds like an important mission," replied Jhin, the silver-haired sniper who was sitting in a corner of the room, exuding confidence. "There's a stray cat that's taken up residence in the Imperial capital. Finding its parents takes top priority."

"I'm not talking about stray cats!"

"Oh, so stray dogs, then?" he said.

"Just leave that to a humane society! Nene, you were listening, weren't you?" Mismis asked.

"That's right. I heard it all." Nene, the red-haired girl sitting next to Iska, raised her hand. "I'm also frightened to hear that molestation incidents have been increasing year by year in the capital. If I have to walk around the alleys at night, then—"

"I'm not talking about that, either!"

"Okay, enough joking around. So basically, you want us to run a counteroperation." Jhin leaned back in his chair as he spoke, his tone clearly indicating that he didn't want to participate. "We have no idea when the Imperial forces' security measures might fail. So you want us to play the role of Nebulis assassins and attempt to infiltrate the Imperial base."

They—the three members of Unit 907 and their leader, Commander Mismis—had been assigned to be spies.

"Right, boss?" Jhin said.

"Exactly! HQ set up a prefab base for us to use as training. It's in the business district, where there used to be an empty lot." Commander Mismis pointed at a location on the map. "This is going to be an experiment. We're part of the spy team. We can use any method we want to force our way into the base."

"So anything goes as long as we don't get caught? Well, what if..."

The first thing that sprang to mind for Iska was sneaking in from above. If they used a military helicopter, they could infiltrate the base without worrying about walls. All they would need to do was descend via parachute.

"Of course, we can't use a helicopter, though," he said, shooting his own idea down.

"Sure we can," Mismis replied.

"You can't be serious?!"

"But the base also has a defense team. They didn't tell me how many people would be on it, but it'll be more people than our team."

Even if they got into the base by parachute, they'd likely end up caught by the opposing team.

"...I see. So they want us to figure out how to sneak past the defense team, just like real spies."

"I wonder what equipment the other side will have." Jhin rose from his seat. "Hey, boss, will the defending team have guns and stuff?"

"Of course. Their firearms will be outfitted with rubber bullets, like the ones used for riot suppression. They'll also have access to handcuffs, nets, and traps installed at the base."

As he listened to Commander Mismis make a list, Iska scowled slightly. "This sounds like it's going to be tough... So the defense team will have anything they need at their disposal, while we'll be limited."

For example, Iska was a swordsman. While the Imperial forces primarily used guns, he specialized in close combat with blades. His skill set wouldn't be useful for this training exercise. In fact, his swords would be far too conspicuous if he brought them along on their stealth mission.

"Commander, do you have any other information about the opposing side?"

"No. I asked about it, but all HQ said was that the defending team would have more people, and that they'd have standard Imperial-issued equipment... No different than usual." Commander Mismis gave them all a strained smile.

They were completely cut off from any other intelligence, as though this were a real mission.

"We have three weeks. We're supposed to come up with a plan and execute it in that time."

"Three weeks? That's absurd." Jhin shook his head immediately. "Even the Nebulis intelligence unit hasn't been able to penetrate Imperial security. We couldn't do it in three weeks, even if we went with a reckless approach."

"R-right, but...the training area is a prefab base they had to put together really quickly. And they also pulled together the defense team at the last minute." Commander Mismis clenched her fists, as though trying to motivate herself. "It'll be fine! This is the first time they're trying this, too. The defense team probably has holes in their communication. If we exploit that, we'll win this for sure!"

"Are you sure about that?"

Suddenly, the door flung open.

Someone had overridden the electronic lock.

"A hole in the defense team? Don't think things will be that easy for you!"

They heard footsteps ring out through the room as a black-haired woman wearing glasses appeared in front of the unit. The woman, who was as small as Mismis, suddenly smiled.

"Hello, Mismis," she said.

"Oh, it's you, P. How have you been?"

"Who are you calling P?!"

Commander Pilie Commonsense.

She was a young member of the Imperial forces who had been promoted only a year ago. Her black hair and well-to-do appearance made her look like a quintessential member of the Imperial capital's upper class. However...

"Her abilities are bottom-tier. Her grades are among the lowest of all the Imperial commanders. She's got more ambition than anyone, and she puts up a good front. But as soon as you peer below the surface, she's just—"

"Hey! Why are you going over my history?! And why are you doing it using an explanatory tone?!"

"She even looks childish, and her appearance is nothing to write home about. But our boss is the only person in the Imperial forces of similar height and academic standing to Commander Pilie, so she's decided they're rivals."

"Stop it already!"

"I'm just stating the facts," Jhin said brazenly when Commander Pilie pointed a finger at him. "I'm pretty sure that was all true."

"Sh-shut up! My looks are a sore spot… At least call me cute instead of childish!" Strangely, Commander Pilie was willing to admit that Jhin's assessment was the truth, though she still turned bright red.

"Ahem. Anyway, back to the topic at hand… I heard everything you said earlier, Mismis!"

"You mean what we were just discussing?"

"That's right, I heard you talking about the training exercise. It seems like you're hoping oversights will save your hide when you try to penetrate the base's defense." Her eyes glinted. She took a large step forward with her little legs. "But don't count on it! Because, I, Commander Pilie, was selected as the general commander of the defense team!"

"…What did you just say?" Iska couldn't help but exclaim in surprise. "Is that true, Commander Pilie?"

"Heh-heh, I see you're so alarmed that your jaws are hanging open!"

The commander was assured of her victory.

Meanwhile, Iska, Commander Mismis, Nene, and Jhin had formed a huddle.

"Wow, I can't believe that happened. Commander, we've basically got a win in the bag now."

"Right? I feel so relieved."

"I'm kind of disappointed," Nene said. "Forget looking for holes—there's a huge one right there!"

"This is like a minigame," Jhin said. "A little kid—no, a mutt—could break right through Commander Pilie's defenses."

"What are the four of you doing?!" Commander Pilie butted into their conversation. "I'm leading the defense team. You're supposed to be despairing right now! Why do you all look relieved?!"

"Thank you, P…"

"You're thanking me now?! Ugh! If you don't get it even after I've spelled it out for you, you can see how terrifying it'll be when we start!" the lead commander of the defense team declared as she gritted her teeth. "Compared to the thirty spies on your side, we've got three hundred people on the defense team. And we won't let a single one of you rats get in!"

"Wow… So you've got three hundred people," Mismis murmured. HQ had withheld that information.

Commander Pilie had divulged some critical information right from the start, but naturally, she hadn't realized that.

"This is the end of the line for you, Mismis. We've been competing for a while now, but this is going to decide it all," Commander Pilie coolly declared. "My defense will be impenetrable. See if you can break through it!"

"Cool." Jhin nodded and confidently accepted the challenge. "Then we'll start tomorrow."

"What did you say?"

"The forces are huge, so they've gotta get lots of food deliveries. You should know that already. We'll disguise ourselves as lunch delivery workers tomorrow and sneak in that way. Try to catch us if you can."

"Sounds interesting to me!" Commander Pilie shouted with a competitive look in her eye. "I can only compliment you for the advance notice and your boldness in divulging your plans...but even if you have professional disguises, you'll never be able to get past my discerning eyes!"

"Yeah, you better be ready for what we throw at you," Jhin said.

"That's exactly what I was hoping for. Well then, Mismis, I'm looking forward to our showdown!"

"Oh...wait, P!"

"Adieu!"

Mismis had no time to stop her. The black-haired commander left the conference room like a speeding arrow.

2

The next day.

In other words, it was the day of Jhin's plan. The Imperial capital had been hit with an unusually heavy rain.

Now, as for what Iska and the gang were doing...

"It sure is pouring outside. Hey, Iska, that window over there looks like a waterfall's running down it," Nene remarked.

"It really does. Good thing we're just doing indoor training today."

They were relaxing in the same conference room as the day before while holding a strategy meeting about their covert operation.

"Say, Jhin."

"Hm? What is it, boss?"

As Jhin took a swig from his can of coffee, Commander Mismis pointed at the wall clock.

"It's almost lunchtime..."

"Yeah, that's obvious."

"What about all the stuff you said to Commander Pilie? Like, about disguising ourselves as lunch delivery workers? If we're going to do that, we need to start now."

"Oh, that." Jhin took another sip of his coffee and answered her with a straight face. "That was a joke, obviously. Who'd take that seriously?"

"Oh, right, of course."

"Yeah, it's a no-brainer. Thirty spies against a three-hundred-person defense team? That's a factor of ten. We were already at a disadvantage to start with. Why would I reveal our plans on purpose?"

"Oh, good. I was almost convinced that you might have been serious." Commander Mismis looked relieved. "P seemed like she was weirdly fired up about it, though. You don't think she actually believed it...?"

"No way. It was tit for tat. I cracked a joke, so she just went along with it. That's all it was."

He tossed the empty can. After it landed in the wastebasket, he let out an exasperated sigh.

"It's not like anyone can become an Imperial commander. No one in a position of leadership would take that baloney seriously."

"Yeah, you're right," Mismis said.

"Obviously."

Everyone there was convinced of that, and the day passed without incident.

The next day.

"...At least that's what we thought."

"You big fat liars!" Commander Pilie ran into the conference room, her face bright red.

"I didn't think anyone would take it seriously," Jhin said.

"Wh-why did you just sigh like that?! Do you have any idea how many hours I spent waiting in the rain for you to break in yesterday night?"

She sneezed.

Evidently, the group leader of the defense team had caught a cold.

"I was guarding the base outside all night. You said you'd come in as food delivery workers, so I was keeping an eye out for you the whole time!"

"That must have been a lot of effort… Wait? You were keeping guard? Don't tell me you did something to the delivery workers—"

"We arrested every single one of them, of course. We handcuffed them and everything."

She'd just dropped a bombshell.

"I took every single female delivery worker and checked everything they had on them, including their IDs. Then I had them undress in a changing room and did a strip search, too."

"Hey, you can't drag citizens into this when they're not part of the exercise."

"I only did it because of what you said!" Pilie shrieked. "We had complaints come in from restaurants all over the capital! Thanks to you, I had to pull an all-nighter writing self-reflection reports. HQ even told me off. How could you do that to me?!"

"Uh, what am I supposed to do about that…?" Jhin shook his head, looking and sounding exasperated. "I'm just glad we weren't real spies."

"What?"

"A Nebulis spy could definitely leak false info to you. You should be thankful you got some practice dealing with that through us."

"I—I suppose you have a point!" Commander Pilie swallowed her breath. "Did you do that on purpose as a learning experience…?"

"No, I was surprised you took me seriously. I didn't think you'd actually believe in it."

"Well then, this means war!"

She pointed at Jhin. Then she howled, turning red from rage and her intense cold.

"I made a mistake this time, but you'll regret angering me. Now that I'm actually going all-out for real, there won't be a single blind spot in my defensive line!" she said through gritted teeth as she firmly made her declaration of war. "You'd better be ready for this, Mismi…achoo!"

"P, you've caught a cold from being in the rain yesterday."

"And whose fault do you think that is?!"

A few days passed.

Unit 907 was in the woods at the edge of the capital. It was late at night.

"So the base that we're targeting as spies is somewhere in this Imperial forest reserve."

Iska was leading the group. Behind him were Commander Mismis, Jhin, and Nene.

"But, Commander, we haven't decided how we're getting in, have we?" Iska said.

"That's right. We're just scouting it really quick today."

There were two routes by which Unit 907 could infiltrate the base. They could either go through the business district of the capital and attack head-on, or attack from the woods and break into the base from behind.

"But this seems really sudden..."

Iska and the others had only been told they would be scouting that night. Per Mismis's orders, Iska was carrying a map and a headlamp, while Jhin and Nene were taking along binoculars and cameras. Commander Mismis herself was dressed in light clothing and carrying a comm.

"Hey, Commander, I'd like to ask you something. What are you using that comm for?" Nene tilted her head. "We're all here, so who else would we need to talk to?"

"Oh, did I not tell you?" Commander Mismis replied nonchalantly. "We're helping one of my friends today."

"A friend?"

"That's right. Someone else from the spy group." Commander Mismis nodded confidently and pulled out the comm. "Another team is going to infiltrate the base tonight. They'll have ten people in total. And they'll go through the woods to get to the base."

"Oh, I see." Iska nodded. He'd assumed the scouting mission was totally spontaneous, but it seemed that the point had been to support another group all along. "So, Commander, what happens if the other group gets into the base successfully?"

"That means the entire spy team has won. If that happens, our training will be over on the spot, so we've got to support them with everything we have!" Commander Mismis parted the underbrush and headed deeper into the woods. "C'mon, you can do it, everybody else!"

"I don't normally condone relying on others, but this time I'm in full agreement. There'd be nothing better than getting this training exercise over with as soon as possible." Jhin held up his binoculars. "Boss, when's the other unit making their move?"

"They should be starting soon. Let me get in contact with them."

The commander pulled out the comm again.

"This is Unit 907's commander, Mismis. We're getting closer to execution time. What's the situation there?"

"Unit 31 commander, Nagra, here. We've rendezvoused with Unit 602."

A sober man's voice came over the comm. They could hear the other members of the unit in the background as Commander Nagra spoke. Ten members of the spy group would be participating in the infiltration. Apparently, they were already on standby.

"Where are you now?"

"We're waiting at the rendezvous point. Right now we're at the environmental conservation boundary's 'forest bear checkpoint,' and we'll be heading to the 'forest rabbit checkpoint' next. It should take us about an hour to reach the rear side of the enemy base. Then it's showtime."

The commanders were using code words.

They'd designated the "forest bear" and "forest rabbit" checkpoints ahead of time to ensure the mission would be a success. The attacking team had opted to use code words to prevent Pilie's group from eavesdropping and deducing their location.

"Hey, Iska, 'forest bear' is a pretty cute code word, isn't it?"

"I dunno. What if you actually get mauled by a bear in the woods...?"

"Shh! Iska, Nene, quiet. They're about to head out!"

Mismis pointed into the trees. They could just barely make out people sneaking through the woods through their night-vision binoculars.

"Looks like they're in camo. The infiltration team did a great job dressing for this." Jhin sounded impressed. "If they can get to the back of the base, I can't wait to see how they deal with the wire on the concrete wall."

They were heading toward a wall equipped with security cameras, where there would also be patrolling soldiers.

How were they planning to get through the defenses with just ten people?

"So what's our job here, Commander?"

"We just need to stay on standby." She brought her comm to her ear. **"Hello? How's it going?"**

"This is Unit 31. Progress going well down the forest route," Commander Nagra answered.

They heard the unit's footsteps parting the undergrowth.

"Uh, um. Good luck out there."

"Ha-ha, Commander Mismis. You worry too much."

The commander let out a hearty laugh. Even though it actually fell to his team to execute the spy mission, he sounded quite confident.

"We won't run into any issues with Commander Pilie leading the team at the base."

"You know her?"

"Yup. She's basically the only commander in history who flubbed her first day on the job. She had to write a self-reflection report."

"Oh, I actually had to do that, too..."

"Hm?"

"Oh, nothing! Ah-ha-ha-ha. Right, no one would have to write a self-reflection report their first day!"

"That's for sure. An elite combo unit like us wouldn't lose to the defenses set up by a woman who just squeaked by as a commander. Right, everyone?"

They heard laughter through the comm. It wasn't just Commander Nagra. Everyone seemed to be chuckling on the other side of the line, as though the mission had practically been handed to them.

"You can rest easy knowing that we've got this."

He seemed very reassuring when he put it like that.

"Oh, um...but have you taken any countermeasures? P is really motivated, after all."

"Ha-ha-ha. Don't worry, Commander Mismis. No matter how much spirit she has, she's still a fail—"

Boom!

Just then, they heard an explosion on the other end of the comm.

"Gaah?!"

Then they heard a scream.

"Uh...Commander?! Commander Nagra?! What happened?!"

"———"

Communication cut off.

"Iska, over there!" Nene pointed in the direction the unit had been walking.

They looked through their night-vision binoculars. White clouds of pillowy smoke were obscuring the thickets.

"Looks like tear gas-firing equipment. It was hidden in the brush." Jhin looked through his binoculars. "That's not all. I don't see anyone coming out of the gas cloud, so there must have been pit hole traps there, too. I bet Commander Nagra's team fell into them."

"P-pit holes?! Are you telling me they walked into a trap?!" Commander Mismis went pale. "But, Jhin, this is meant to be a conservation zone. They couldn't have been there originally..."

"The defense team must have dug them for this training exercise."

"During the last few days?!" Mismis spoke into the comm. **"Commander Nagra, please answer!"**

"Ugh…th-they got us! It was a tear gas trap!"

Iska and the others watched as a large man leaped out from a cloud of tear gas, looking like he was in pain.

"And there are pits all over the place! It was a bloodbath… My whole team—all nine of my troops—got caught!"

"Wh-what?!"

"I never expected her to be so prepared…but I'm still here!"

Perhaps spurred by his sense of duty as an Imperial soldier, or the fact that he couldn't allow himself to be beaten by a young girl, Commander Nagra ran right through the tear gas. He was still heading for the base.

"Sh-shouldn't you withdraw?!" Mismis asked.

"Leave this to me. It's pitch black. No one can see me with camo—"

Flick.

Just then, an intense spotlight shone on Commander Nagra.

"I-impossible! An infrared tracking system?!" he screamed.

This was no normal infrared surveillance camera. It was bona fide Imperial forces equipment.

"I can't believe it. How much of the budget did Pilie blow on this?!"

"Commander Nagra?!"

"Urgh!"

He ran through the vegetation, but the surveillance equipment followed him wherever he went. And then…

A gigantic net fell on him from above.

"Gaaaaah!"

"Commander, Commander, keep it together!"

Mismis frantically called out to him, only to receive silence on the other end.

"———"

A few moments later, they finally heard his sad voice over the comm.

"...I'm sorry, Commander Mismis."

"Commander Nagra?"

"It seems this is where we say goodbye. We've all been wiped out."

"Wh-what?! Commander, you can't—"

"Be careful out there. That young lady isn't the same person she once was... I pray fortune will be in your favor!"

The comm cut off. It must have been intercepted by a jamming radio wave from the base.

"Commander, we need to withdraw. Let's run."

"B-but!—"

"The defense units will come any minute. We'll go down like them if we stick around. Don't waste their sacrifice!"

"Urgh. I-I'm sorry, Commander, and the rest of you!" Mismis cried out like a heroine in a story, wiping away her tears and running after Iska.

"This is so unfair of the defense team! How could they use so much of their budget to protect the base?! How are we supposed to even try tackling that?!"

"...You got over everything that happened real quick."

"That's because they're not playing fair!" Mismis wailed.

They ran through the dark woods.

The spy group had lost ten of its members, but Unit 907 managed to escape under the direction of Commander Mismis.

3

Three days passed.

"Everyone else was taken out..." Commander Mismis gave the rest of her team the news in a heavy tone in a conference room. "They got two whole units. The offensive team was able to infiltrate the woods, but there was so much surveillance and so many traps that they had no place to step."

"The team at the base put a ridiculous amount of effort into this." Jhin leaned back in his chair. "They've really tightened their defenses. We'll need to take this seriously if we want to stand a chance."

"Any good ideas, Jhin?"

"Zilch. If I've got to say anything, it's that attacking through the woods is hopeless."

"Which means..." Commander Mismis breathed in sharply. "What about the front route?"

"Right. And dressed up as citizens. In plainclothes without any equipment."

"D-do you think that'll work...?"

"I think that's the only option we've got," Nene said. She unfurled a map of the Imperial capital. "This is Commander Pilie we're talking about. She'll have metal detectors prepared. We'll get caught if we have comms or binoculars."

"All right. We'll go ahead with the plan under the assumption that we need to be dressed as civilians."

First, they would disguise themselves. Then they would walk right through the Imperial capital and march up to the front gate of the base.

But that's when things would get tricky.

"So, Jhin, what happens after we get to the front gate?"

"We'll break in through sheer willpower."

"Why's that the only part of the plan that relies on brute force?!"

"What else are we supposed to do?" Jhin asked. "Look how tough their defense is in the back area by the woods. We've got to use the front route. It's a no-brainer."

"You have a point, but—"

"The alternative is to use a decoy. While you're hit with the tear gas, boss, the rest of us can try climbing over the wall."

"Don't joke like that! And why am I the decoy?!"

"Isn't it your duty as an officer to sacrifice yourself for the rest of the team, Commander?"

"No way!"

Jhin fixed her with a serious look, and Mismis let out a real shriek.

4

The evening streets were lit with neon. Melting into the bustling crowds, Iska's unit walked through the business district.

"This is finally going to be what decides it..." Commander Mismis had a grim look in her eyes. She had changed out of her battle uniform and donned a cute dress. "There are ten members of the spy group remaining. There are the four of us and another unit of six."

"And the other unit is also carrying out the same plan."

Next to her was Iska, in a plain shirt. Jhin was walking behind him in a similar outfit, and Nene had changed into a skirt that emphasized her youth. They were perfectly disguised. From an objective standpoint, they were indistinguishable from any other group of teenagers in the business district.

"It's a good thing you don't look your age, boss. You look the youngest out of all of us."

"Jhin, I don't just *look* young. I'm twenty-two, so I *am* young. Anyway, we need to get out of the business district. We'll go straight to the Imperial base."

She plowed straight ahead.

Then she pulled a comm out of her pocket.

"This is Commander Mismis of Unit 907. How is it going?"

"This is Commander Wien of Unit 871, Division II. We're also making progress through the business district."

They received a reply through the comm. The spy group had broken up into two teams and were heading for the base from the right and the left.

"We've dressed up as office workers who just finished a day on the job. We're in suits."

"Looks like things are going according to plan."

"That's right. And we made copies of documents from companies that do business with the Imperial forces. Our cover story is that we're about to go in for a meeting with the Imperial forces' general affairs manager."

"Well, if you've gone that far..."

"Yup. That should get us through the front gate, at least."

They were acting like real spies. If they couldn't actually sneak in, then their only option was to try to waltz right through the front doors of the base.

"So the goal is the entrance, right?"

"That's right. If any of us puts a hand on the door, then the spies all win."

"I see. Then we'll make sure to be the decoys for you!"

Mismis's unit was in charge of making a commotion by pretending to be civilians near the wall of the base. Commander Wien's group of six were most likely to be successful.

"Let's do the best we can, Commander Wien!"

"Ha-ha-ha! Leave it to us, Commander Mismis," Wien said, acting like this would be the easiest thing in the world.

However, Commander Mismis started to get anxious when she heard the confidence in his reply.

"B-but Commander Nagra's entire team was wiped out just a few days ago. If you go in with the same attitude they did..."

"Nagra's team was wiped out because they made the mistake of trying to brute-force their way in. Our plan is foolproof."

"...I see."

"That's right. And we're up against Commander Pilie, after all. An elite unit like ours wouldn't lose to a girl like her."

"Uh-huh..."

This conversation gave her a feeling of déjà vu. Iska and the others could still vividly recall how Commander Nagra's pride had led to his unit being wiped out.

"Please be careful!"

"Ha-ha-ha. You worry too much, Commander Mismis. With us dressed up as company employees like this, even God himself couldn't—"

Just then, Wien's voice was replaced by static.

"Huh? Commander Wien?"

"I-impossible!"

They heard panic on the other side of the comm.

"They're jamming the comm?!"

"Ha-ha-ha! You were too naive, Commander Wien! And you too, Mismis!"

A voice that sounded just as childish as Mismis's came over the speakers of the business district.

"We already knew that you ten spies would try to attack tonight!"

"Commander Pilie?!"

She'd tapped Commander Wien's comm.

"This can't be! We only nailed down the details of the plan here. We met in this district and had our briefing while pretending to be office workers. There's no way you could have figured us out!"

"And that's what makes you naive. I knew about the location of the café where you held your planning meeting this whole time."

"What?!"

"Take a closer look around you."

There was a murmur.

Everyone in the crowd around them stopped and turned toward Unit 907.

"They're all Imperial detectives I hired. I had all of them pretend to be regular citizens and tail you the entire time."

"You hired all these people?! Just how big is your budget…?"

"Ah-ha-ha-ha! Did you forget that my family owns a conglomerate?"

Commander Pilie smiled as though she'd already won.

"If I take out the entire spy group here, my reputation at headquarters will soar. If it's for boosting my prestige, I don't mind spending a little cash!"

"Th-that's underhanded! Who would allow you to spend that much money so extravagantly?!"

"In war, a budget speaks volumes. Now, capture them, Defense Team A!"

They heard an explosion on the other side of the comm followed by the sounds of what seemed like death screams.

"Gaaaaah!"

"Commander Wien?!"

"..."

There was no reply.

"C-Commander...Commander?!" Mismis's forlorn cry rang out.

Then, the other commander's final, demoralizing message came through.

"...I'm sorry, Commander Mismis."

"Commander Wien?"

"It seems this is where we say goodbye. We need to drop out of the operation now, but you all keep going. Good luck!"

"Commander Wien?!"

The comm cut off.

After being captured in the business district, the six members of his team must have been taken to the base.

"Ha-ha. We didn't even let them get to the base before capturing them. We caught them on their way there to prevent anyone on the spy team from infiltrating us!" Commander Pilie gloated as though she'd already won. "All right, Mismis, this is when we settle things. We'll leave only the four of you for a fair fight."

"How is this fair, P?!"

"My wits were what brought me this victory!"

"I think money is what bought it for you!"

She'd overwhelmed them not only by relying on her budget from headquarters but also by using her vast amount of personal wealth.

Anything goes, it seemed.

"All right, Defense Team B! Capture Mismis!"

They heard the loud thudding of military boots. Tons of heavily equipped Imperial soldiers filed out of the alleys, surrounding

Iska's unit one after another. There were twenty people—no, more than thirty.

"Run, Commander! They're going to surround us!"

"Uh, uh-huh!"

They dashed as fast as they could through the business district. Naturally, they ran toward the Imperial base, where Commander Pilie was waiting.

"Iska, they're approaching from the front, too!"

"Guh! Nene! Let's escape through that small alleyway!"

It was so narrow, only one person could get through at once. A large crowd wouldn't be able to follow them, so as long as they hid, no one would be able to find them.

"*Haah…haah…* I-isn't this unfair? We've only got four people, but they've got hundreds!"

"Shh, Commander. They'll hear you."

Commander Mismis hid by the wall as Nene checked their surroundings.

"From now on, it's hide-and-seek. We'll just lie low until the defense team starts getting impatient—"

"Hey, wait," Jhin whispered. He stared in the direction of the narrow alley they had come from.

"I heard something."

"What? What did you hear, Jhin?"

"A dog barking."

This wasn't a cute little yelp, either. It was the cry of a large, ferocious dog—the kind that would growl and bare its teeth.

"They've caught their scent!"

Suddenly, a light shined into the alley they were all hiding in. Then they saw a soldier holding not a gun but the leash of a large military canine.

"They're using hounds?!"

"Hey, wait a sec! That's going way too far across the line now!"

Now even Jhin was rushing to get away. There was a military hound after them, after all. No matter where they hid, it would track them if it caught the slightest scent.

"Ahhh?!"

"Nene?!"

"M-my skirt!"

Two dogs had latched on to the hem of Nene's skirt. Her long, slender thighs peeked out from underneath as she pulled it up to shake them off.

"Ahh! Don't look!" Her face was turning redder and redder. "Waaah! I'm not supposed to be the one who's embarrassed like this! That's Commander Mismis's role!"

"What's that supposed to mean, Nene?!"

"Urgh… I really liked this skirt, too…!"

Nene tore through her own skirt with the knife she always carried on her person. Then she ran from the dogs, which were still clinging to the fabric. The entire unit started running through the backstreets again.

"Iska, what do we do?!" Commander Mismis looked behind her. "At this rate, we won't be able to get away! We'll be surrounded before we even get to the base."

"Let's split up."

There was no time to hesitate. Iska pointed at a corner as he made the split-second decision. They could either go straight or turn the corner.

"Jhin and I will run straight. You two sneak around the corner and make a break for it."

"Are you sure, Iska?!"

"Worry about yourself first. Get going, boss, Nene!" Jhin started things off by breaking into a sprint.

Iska followed him. After a beat, Commander Mismis and Nene ran around the corner. However…

““Oh no!”” Jhin and Iska both yelled at the same time.

The hounds and the soldiers of the canine unit had turned the corner and followed the two women instead.

“They're going after Commander Mismis first!”

“Iska, we're going to operate on our own. Run!”

They could only hope that the rest of their unit would make it out safely. Praying that they would meet Nene and Commander Mismis again later, Iska ran from the alleys back into the business district.

“Found you!”

“Guh! We ran right back into them!”

Imperial soldiers resumed their pursuit. However, Iska and Jhin were faster.

“Jhin, they're slow runners.”

“Their equipment is weighing them down. We're dressed lightly, so they won't be able to follow us if we keep running.”

Then something flew right in front of Jhin's nose. As it rushed by, they realized it was a rubber bullet—the kind used to suppress riots—that had barely grazed him. That was forces-issued ammunition.

“They've even got a sniper unit?!” Jhin blanched and shuddered. “They must be on the roof. So the defense team led us into a spot where the snipers would have a good view.”

“Jhin, this way!”

They ran in the shadows of the buildings.

Behind them, the heavily armed defense team continued to give chase. At the same time, military snipers aimed at them from the buildings above.

“This is harder than our usual training!”

“Damn it! How complicated are they going to make this?!”

They headed to the north of the district. Finally, they saw the buildings peter out.

Once they'd cleared the hill, they would get to the base.

"There they are! It's the spy group!" They heard soldiers from behind.

"Sniper unit, aim, Alice—"

"Wait, Alice?!" Iska reflexively turned back when he heard that name. The Ice Calamity Witch Aliceliese. She was the second princess of the Nebulis Sovereignty and Iska's rival in the battlefield. "Alice can't be here, can she?!"

"Iska, don't stop!"

When he heard Jhin, he came back to his senses.

The Ice Calamity Witch Aliceliese wasn't there when Iska had looked. Instead, he saw an Imperial sniper holding a gun.

"That's not the same Alice!"

They scrambled up the hill. The Imperial base came faintly into view, illuminated by spotlights that were always on.

"Iska, Jhin!"

"Nene?! You made it out okay?"

Nene and Commander Mismis were running up the hill, too. Iska was relieved that they were fine, but then he heard the vehement howl of hounds behind them.

"Ah?! We worked so hard to shake them off, but the canine unit is still behind us!"

"Nene, hurry!"

The four of them reunited. Once they ran up the hill, they found that the automatic doors were closing on them.

"The doors!"

"Jump!"

They tumbled in, slipping through the gap in the entrance to infiltrate the base.

"All right! Everyone, if we touch that door, we win!" Mismis took a step forward.

"Wait, boss!" Jhin grabbed Mismis's hand to stop her.

"Wh-what's wrong, Jhin...?"

"Look closer. There are unnatural mounds all over the lawn."

"What?"

"Let me show you what they are." Jhin picked up a pebble and threw it onto the lawn.

Blip.

They heard a soft electrical sound.

Whoom! The lawn exploded, sending up a gigantic shower of dirt.

"L-land mines?!"

"They're buried all over the place. If you run straight ahead, you'll definitely step on one."

"Ha-ha-ha." They heard a familiar voice echo throughout the base's speakers. **"Great job making it this far after overcoming all those trials. No wonder you're my archnemesis, Mismis."**

It was the leader of the defense team, Pilie. She was likely watching them from afar through a surveillance camera.

"But the party's over. You'll be blown to beautiful pieces here."

Whoooom...

They felt something move as a gigantic shadow descended over the back of the base.

"I'm making a personal appearance for the grand finale."

"That's a tank!"

It was the Imperial army's UTV-70X model tank. It was equipped with a heavy machine gun that could riddle a building with holes within seconds and an automobile combat defense system.

"Well, Mismis." Pilie's voice blared from the tank. Needless to say, she had to be the person driving it. **"We'll settle this the customary way!"**

"How is pitting a tank against humans customary?!"

"In war, the battle is over before the fighting even begins. The real thrill of the battle is thoroughly preparing yourself."

"Then what about our 'customary' battle?"

"I just want to win!"

"*Now* you admit it?!"

"En guarde!"

The tank began to move without another word. The gigantic caterpillar track started to turn, trampling the lawn as the vehicle charged forward.

"Whoa! It's heading straight for us, Iska!"

"What are you going to try to do to us when we're unarmed?! Do something, Commander!"

"I can't do anything!"

"All we can do is run!"

They all did just that and sprinted as fast as they could. There was no way that unarmed humans could win against a cutting-edge tank.

"This is bad, Commander. There's a wall in front of us. We're cornered!"

"Are we done for?!"

The unit gathered at the dead end. Pilie was approaching them in her tank.

"All right, just accept defeat. This is definitive proof of the difference between us."

"You mean the difference between humans and a tank?!"

"That works, too. As long as I win—"

Click.

They heard the sound of the tank rolling over something as it approached.

Bip, bip, bip.

A familiar electrical sound rang out.

"Oh?" Pilie seemed confused.

Iska and the others stared at the tank. It was sitting right on top of a mound of dirt containing something they'd already encountered.

"C'mon…"

"P, you didn't…"

They had a bad feeling about this.

The tank hadn't just rolled over one land mine. All four caterpillar tracks were right on top of separate mounds.

"H-how could this happen?! I rolled right on top of the land mines I set up myself!"

"I knew it!"

"What are you doing, P?!"

"Why'd you get yourself caught in your own trap?! Run, they're going to explode!"

Iska and the rest of his team dashed off as fast as they could.

"W-wait a second! Don't leave me here! Uh, ah, noooo!"

Then they exploded, and spectacularly at that.

Leaving only a sad wail in her wake, Commander Pilie and her tank went flying into the air.

5

The next day.

In a room in the Nebulis Sovereignty, far, far away from the Empire.

"There was a giant explosion in the Imperial capital?" Alice said as she read a magazine that her attendant, Rin, had prepared for her.

Aliceliese Lou Nebulis. She was a princess who was feared by the Empire for being one of the strongest witches around.

"Rin, tell me the details."

"Yes, Lady Alice, the origin of the explosion was within an Imperial base." Rin looked nervous. "It seems that it was some sort of accident. There are eyewitness reports of a tank moving in the vicinity of the base. People think it went out of control..."

"No, Rin, you need to look deeper," Alice declared with confidence as she held the magazine in hand. "That was a trap. That was likely a test explosion that they made to look like the tank self-destructing. The Imperial forces must be testing a secret weapon they've developed."

"Wh-what?!"

"There's no way that the forces would make such a silly mistake and blow themselves up. Especially not with Iska serving them."

Iska, the former Saint Disciple. Alice couldn't believe the swordsman who'd entranced her on the battlefield could work for an organization that would blow themselves up.

"The Empire truly is a cunning enemy. We'll likely have even more intense battles with them going forward..."

She was completely convinced that the Empire couldn't be so incompetent. Alice renewed her vow to overthrow their enemy.

"Just you wait, Iska!"

Meanwhile, at the same time...

"It burned down..."

"The land mines blew the whole thing up. The prefab base is gone."

"I can't believe we survived that..."

The Imperial capital Yunmelngen.

In a daze, Iska and the rest of his unit stared at the base that had burned to cinders.

It was their day off. But Iska and the others held brooms and dustpans in their hands.

"They're making both the spy group and the defense team clean up together..."

"Geez. We're losing a perfectly good day off."

"It's all because P went too far."

"Nuh-uh! It's because you guys were too tenacious!" Commander Pilie was wrapped in bandages.

"P, why don't you just rest? Those burns must hurt," Mismis said.

"Shut up... I've gotta help clean up as the general commander."

Commander Pilie was hard at work cleaning with them. She'd been injured after the land mine blast, but she was also the first to have started cleaning because she was responsible for the incident.

"This loss is also a learning experience. Just you wait. I won't lose to you next time, Mismis."

Pilie pouted, and Mismis stared at her from the side for a while.

"You're so adorable, P," she finally concluded.

"What?!"

"That's the one aspect of you that's impossible to hate."

Mismis smiled awkwardly.

File 03

Our Last Crusade or the Turbulent Halloween Party

Our Last CRUSADE OR THE RISE OF A New World

Secret File

CONFIDENTIAL

1

The witch's paradise—also known as the Nebulis Sovereignty.

The Nebulis Palace.

"No more! I can't do this anymore!" Alice yelled in front of the mountains of paperwork. "It's been a whole week straight of this. It feels like my entire job is sitting in my study and signing my name! It's so boring that I'm groggy, and my back and buttocks hurt from sitting for so long!"

Aliceliese Lou Nebulis. She was the Sovereignty's second princess, and her brilliant golden hair complemented her charming features. Despite her gorgeous appearance, she was currently wailing and on the verge of tears.

"Look at this, Rin! I've held this pen for so long that my fingers are red and swollen!"

"Signing documents is one of your duties as a princess," her attendant, Rin, said bluntly. She was also Alice's guard.

"Say, Rin, don't you feel sorry that a young girl like me is suffering from stiff shoulders and back pain?"

"Not at all."

"Well, you should! At least let me take a break. I want to stretch my wings outside the palace. Let's go out somewhere!"

"All right," Rin said. "I'll make the arrangements."

"I knew it, you'd never allow it. All right, all right. You don't need to tell me…wait?" Alice's eyes went wide, and her eyelashes fluttered once she'd processed Rin's unexpected reply. "Rin, what did you…?"

"If you would like to go on an outing, then I shall make the arrangements. I think I know something quite suitable."

"Suitable for me?" Alice confirmed.

"We can go to a carnival."

Rin pulled out a schedule book, checking Princess Alice's official appearances.

"It's somewhat similar to Halloween," Rin continued. "Sightseers from all over dress up and participate in a parade at a carnival."

"Where is it?"

"Do you know of the city-state of Bachils?"

"Aren't they aligned with the Empire?!" Alice asked, unintentionally raising her voice. The Empire was one of the two global superpowers, and it was locked in an ongoing war with the Sovereignty. Its citizens called those like Alice witches, in a derogatory sense.

The nation Rin had mentioned was affiliated with the Empire.

"Bachils is a small country that derives most of its income from tourism. They'll be holding a carnival next week."

"But, Rin, an enemy state would be much too dangerous to visit, even during a time of revelry."

Since Bachils was a tourist country, it would likely have lax immigration checks. However, if anyone found out Alice was a witch princess, she would doubtlessly be attacked. She could even run into Imperial soldiers there.

"Rest assured that our only goal is to participate in the carnival."

"So we're not going there to fight?"

"That's right, we're not. A large number of sightseers will be dressing up at the carnival for the parade. Since our faces will be obscured, we will be able to walk through the city in the open. It's perfect for observing the enemy."

"Oh, I see. You're right."

It was an important task in its own way. They would participate in the enemy's carnival and observe them. Whatever the case, Alice preferred it to being cooped up in her study.

"What will we wear to it?"

"You can rent outfits at the location. I will prepare costumes for both of us. Do you have any requests?"

"Since we're dressing up, I'd like something flashy."

As long as Alice's face was covered, no one would know she was a Sovereignty princess.

But there was something that bothered her.

"Say, Rin, Bachils is still affiliated with an enemy. Do you think the Imperial forces will be there, too?"

"Even if they are, there will only be a few representatives. The chances of coming across them at a costume carnival are low."

"Do you think Iska will be there as well?"

"Excuse me? Lady Alice, what was that?"

"N-no, nothing!"

She had accidentally said the name of a swordsman who was part of the Imperial forces.

Iska, the Saint Disciple. He was the only person Alice had ever fought to a draw in the battlefield—and he was her rival. She had decided they would settle things someday.

"Will Iska be dispatched there, too?" She stared out the window as she murmured to herself.

2

The largest military state in the world, the Empire.

Inside an Imperial military base.

"Everyone, we've got a trip coming up on the weekend."

"You mean working security at the carnival? I remember, but it's a pretty unusual mission." Iska, the black-haired swordsman, turned to the commander. "We're being dispatched to Bachils?"

"That's right. We're supposed to dress up in costumes and blend in at the carnival." Commander Mismis nodded. Though she had a baby face and a child's stature, she was an Imperial commander and a member of the forces.

"Hey, Commander? What are we supposed to do while we're there?" In the corner of the conference room, a red-haired girl named Nene suddenly rose from her chair. "So we dress up like we're tourists...and then we help guard the carnival? Does that mean we'll be rounding up rowdy drunks or something?"

"That's the job of the military police on the scene. It's not our jurisdiction," Jhin, the silver-haired sniper, replied.

The swordsman Iska, Commander Mismis, Nene, and Jhin made up a four-person unit.

"If the Imperial forces need to be there, that means we'll be going up against astral mages. Did we get intel that they're sending spies in?"

"You're right. That's exactly what's going on." Commander Mismis nodded at Jhin's question. "And it happened last year, too.

There were some suspicious tourists at the carnival who we believe were Sovereignty witches on an espionage mission."

"Aha, I see. So that's why we're being sent in… But that seems like a challenge." Iska sighed after imagining the bustling crowd at the carnival.

Bachils's carnival was known for attracting tens of thousands of visitors. Trying to find a spy in that mess would be like attempting to locate a single ant in a vast desert.

"It'll be difficult finding them and even worse trying to capture them."

"Sheesh. And you want even me and Iska to dress up? That's way too much work, c'mon." Jhin leaned back in his chair and sighed at the task at hand. "So then what? What are we gonna wear?"

"I have the catalog," Nene said. "Here, Jhin!"

She pulled a thick book out of her bag.

"Here, this is it! The most popular costume is this black wide-brimmed hat to dress as a witch, and the second most popular is a fiend. And they've got really realistic mummies and zombies on the next page!"

"All of these are monster costumes."

"Well, it's a costume carnival. What'll you wear, Iska? I think this werewolf would work for you."

"Me? I dunno… I've never attended one of these before."

There were dozens of sample costumes. Settling on one would be difficult.

"It's probably better to hide our faces, so the spies don't find out we're there."

Suddenly, an idea came to Iska. He wondered who the spies from the Sovereignty would be. If they needed to blend in with the carnival, they probably wouldn't look like stereotypical witches. He imagined the spies would be beautiful young women.

......Like...

......Alice, for example?

The Ice Calamity Witch Aliceliese, whom Iska had fought on the battlefield. Alice was an enemy princess, but if she concealed her identity, she could have worked as a model anywhere in the world.

"She would shine at the carnival...but there's no way she'd be there."

Iska shook his head and focused on choosing his costume.

3

A plaza in the city-state of Bachils.

The day of the carnival.

In this country of only twelve streets, people were already flooding the roads before sunrise.

"Wh-wh-what is this getup?!"

They were in a palatial women's changing room. Alice couldn't help but shout when she looked at the clothes Rin had handed her.

"You never told me about this. What are these...these bandage-like things?!"

"Those aren't bandage-like, they *are* bandages."

"But why?!"

"Because you're a mummy girl," Rin answered as she got into her own costume.

"A mummy is a type of horror monster that's wrapped up in bandages. It's popular to dress up as scary things for the carnival. Reference the model in the catalog to see how it should look."

"This girl is only wearing bandages, though! Where are the rest of her clothes...?"

"Yes, the costume is just bandages. Why would a mummy wear a skirt?"

"What?!"

The "mummy girl" in the costume catalog was wearing only underwear and bandages on top of her bare skin.

"If the people discover that a princess such as myself wore such a scandalous outfit..."

"You're the one who asked for something 'flashy,' Lady Alice. You wanted to stand out."

"This is going too far!" she quivered.

Meanwhile, Rin was wearing black wings and a tail as part of her devil costume. She looked adorable and didn't need to show much skin. She wouldn't feel embarrassed at all being seen in her outfit.

"Rin, that's unfair! I'm going to exchange mine for the same costume as yours!"

"Unfortunately, the last day you could cancel your order was yesterday. There are tens of thousands participating in the carnival, so the management said it would be too difficult to handle costume changes on the day of."

"Wh-what...? Urgh!"

There was a line for the changing room. If they stayed too long, they would be inconveniencing others. Alice steeled herself and grabbed the edge of her dress.

"F-fine! I'll dress as a mummy girl, if that's what you want!"

She changed into nothing but her undergarments. When the other girls around her saw her body, they started to stir.

They were stunned. Her breasts seemed on the verge of spilling out of her underwear. Her slender stomach curved out into hips that demanded one's attention. Alice's well-developed body quickly drew the eyes of those around her.

......I—I feel kind of embarrassed.

......I need to change fast!

She wrapped the bandages around her just like the model in the catalog. Despite how awkward she felt, she finished wrapping her arms and legs, then started on the next region. However...

"Oh no......"

"What is it, Lady Alice?"

"This is a crisis, Rin." Alice pointed at her own much-too-large chest.

Her bust was so prominent that she was having trouble wrapping it. When she tried, the bandages fell off, and she could already tell she wouldn't have enough fabric.

"Rin, are you sure you didn't order the mummy costume in your size?"

"Yes. Is there something wrong?"

"I don't have enough fabric to wrap my chest. I wonder if it's because we're such different sizes."

"What's that supposed to mean?!"

"See, I can't wrap my buttocks, either. Actually..."

She stared at her attendant. Compared to an early bloomer like Alice, Rin was very petite. Her guard training had given her the body of an athlete.

"I wonder if this might fit you better. Your bust and buttocks are practically flat, after all."

"Is it a crime to have a small chest?!"

"It's a compliment. You seem like you'd be able to wear these bandages with ease."

"That's not any compliment I'm happy to receive! Wait, what are you doing, Lady Alice?!"

"We're trading, that's what we're doing!"

She caught Devil Rin.

"You can see it's impossible for me to fit in that mummy outfit. In that case, the only thing we can do is trade."

"Wh-what?!"

"Rin, take off your clothes!"

"Stoppp!"

Ten minutes later, Rin had transformed into a magnificent, bright red mummy.

Though her bust and butt were hidden by bandages, her taut stomach peeked from between the gaps. She had an entirely different physique.

"Urgh… I—I can't believe I have to walk around town in such an embarrassing outfit… Lady Alice, this is torture!"

"You were the one trying to subject your own lady to this experience!"

On the other hand, Alice had transformed into a cute devil.

"Let's head out, Rin. We'll join the parade first. And I'd like to participate in the costume contest in the afternoon. By entering you."

"Me?!"

"Of course. That mummy costume is sure to be a hit."

"Wait just one moment!"

Two girls stood in Alice's way.

"We can't let that go after you said that," one of the two strangers said.

"You think you'll be a big hit at the costume contest?" the other girl asked. "With us entering?"

One was a golden-haired girl dressed as a vampire. The other was going as a succubus with black hair. Neither of the costumes was a rental; they looked custom-made. Because they were handmade, there was a freshness and completeness to them that the rental costumes lacked.

"Are you specialists or something?" Rin furrowed her brows when she saw the execution of their costumes. "Lady Alice, these two must be pro cosplayers."

"Cosplayers?"

"They're probably models hired on by the people running the event to make it more festive."

Of course. Alice wasn't very familiar with the term, but the two women were very cute in their costumes. The one dressed as a vampire was even wearing fake fangs, which looked extra impressive because they were covered in what looked like real blood. The other woman was the spitting image of a succubus, and her getup emphasized her unashamedly exposed cleavage.

If those two entered the parade, they were sure to become the center of attention.

"So what does a pair of pros want with us?" Alice wouldn't lose to them, however. With her strikingly good looks and glamorous proportions, it would be no exaggeration to say she stood above the rest of the participants. "Rin and I are just here to enjoy the carnival. Is there something wrong?"

"I'll give you a warning out of goodwill. It appears as though you're newbies dressed in costume rentals. Are you here for Twelfth Street's costume contest?"

"Yes, that's right."

"Ah-ha! Ah-ha-ha!"

"How hilarious!"

The pair's laughter echoed in the changing room.

"The entire world is watching this carnival. And Twelfth Street's costume contest is a super-elite competition designed for pro cosplayers like us."

"That's right. If you're planning to use rentals, then maybe you should enter the Second Street beginner competition?"

"What was that?"

Had the women suggested that in good faith, Alice would have listened to them, but they were clearly looking down on her and Rin.

"I won't deny that we're new to this," Alice said, "but don't you dare underestimate us."

"Hmm? Well, it does look like you've got some assets under your devil costume," the vampire said, appraising Alice after looking her up and down.

"But that still won't work. The makeup's so bad, it looks like a kid put your outfit together."

"We spent a ton of time on handmaking our costumes and researching what makeup to use. We wouldn't want some amateurs tarnishing the reputation of the contest."

The differences in their costumes and makeup were evident. However, it wasn't in the Nebulis princess's nature to back down from a challenge.

"All right. Now that you've said that, I'm fired up to participate!" Alice pointed a finger at the two women. "I accept your challenge! On Rin's behalf!"

"Why me?!"

"I'm a princess; I can't attract attention." Alice grabbed Rin's hand and marched them out the door of the changing room. "Now, Rin, let's go to the contest entry desk as fast as we can make it."

"Lady Alice, w-wait a second. If we go too fast, my bandages will unravel!"

At the same time, on Bachil's Twelfth Street.

"How is it, Commander? Is it cute?"

"You're adorable, Nene!"

Nene had transformed into a cat, complete with ears, a tail, and toe bean gloves. Commander Mismis stood beside her, positively delighted by the costume.

"Ugh! I can't get enough of those gloves and those cat ears! Nene, say 'Meow'!"

"Me-meow! I'm just kitten around!"

"Too cute!" Commander Mismis hugged Nene. The girl started to wriggle around like an actual cat, looking the picture of cuteness.

"You're adorable, Commander. That huge hat looks great on you!"

"Hee-hee, thank you, Nene!"

Commander Mismis was dressed like a witch. The large hat and robe looked great on her small body.

In reality, *witch* was a derogatory term. The Imperials called the Nebulis astral mages "witches" to condemn them, so it was ironic that dressing as one was popular in an affiliate of the Empire.

"Nene, let's take pictures at that studio over there to remember this!"

"Sounds paw-fect to me!"

"You two are really getting into your roles…"

Nene and Commander Mismis were already in the carnival spirit as Iska and Jhin emerged from the men's changing room. They seemed unsteady on their feet.

Their costumes interfered with their vision and were difficult to walk in.

"Those outfits look great on you two," Iska commented. "How are you doing, Jhin?"

"Sheesh. You two seem like you don't have a care in the world. Meanwhile, we're dressed in all this stuff."

Next to Iska was the sniper, Jhin. But their costumes hid both of their faces.

"Um, who are you?" Mismis asked.

"It's me, Iska."

A gigantic dog and rabbit were standing in front of Commander Mismis. Iska was the dog, and Jhin was the rabbit. Though both animals were mascots of the carnival, the costumes were so large that they seemed intimidating.

"We're the carnival's mascots. I'm the dog, Bowell, and Jhin is the rabbit, Rabi."

"Why are you in character costumes?"

"I'm carrying my swords, and Jhin needs to hide his gun. Our only option was to dress as mascots."

They were on the lookout for witches and had to hide their equipment in their costumes so they wouldn't be uncovered as Imperial soldiers.

"Commander, Nene, what about your weapons?"

"We have guns on us, too. I have one under this huge hat."

"The cat's out of the bag," Nene replied. "These paws are packing."

They were equipped even while wearing their witch and cat costumes.

"Nene, how long are you going to make cutesy cat puns?"

"I'm feline like I could do this all day," she replied.

"Okay, I guess it's fine since it's adorable."

Moments earlier, Nene had been waffling about putting the costume on, but now she was fully into her role.

"So, Commander, should we head to the paw-rade, too? Or are we just gonna lo-itter around and guard the town?"

"Right. Okay, let's go. Iska, Jhin, you come, too."

"Whoa? P-please wait, Commander. We can't run in these costumes!"

The streets were bustling with people as they walked.

A girl running down the street in the same direction as Iska ran right at him at the same time.

"Whoa!" Iska exclaimed.

"Ah! I-I'm sorry!"

They brushed by each other slightly.

"Oh, um...pardon me!" the girl said.

She was in a devil costume.

The girl was around the same height as Iska, and her faintly glistening golden hair looked beautiful, but unfortunately, he couldn't see much from within his character suit. On top of that, the little bump had caused the head of the costume to tilt slightly, so he couldn't see the girl's face.

"Lady Alice, you're rushing too much!" Behind the girl dressed as a devil was someone who seemed to be a mummy. "I said it would be dangerous to run."

"Wh-what else am I to do?! The costume contest closes entries in fifteen minutes!"

Wait.

Iska thought he recognized the two girls' voices, but from inside his costume, he could barely make out what they were saying.

"A-anyway, sorry for bumping into you, guy in the dog costume!"

I'm fine, he wanted to say, but he just waved instead.

Iska was wearing the costume of the mascot, Bowell, and the rules of the carnival stipulated that anyone dressed as a mascot needed to remain silent to avoid spoiling the magic.

"Let's hurry, Rin. You're going to win that costume contest."

"That's ridiculous! And don't forget that we're here to gather intel!"

The devil and mummy ran off.

Nene popped her head out from around the corner in front of Iska.

"Hurry up, Iska! There's a ton of people gathered for the paw-rade. We might find some witches in there, so if you see anyone suspicious, make sure to tail us about it right away."

"I know. I don't think they'd be anywhere near us, though."

They lined up for the parade and got going. Then Commander Mismis showed up.

"We're going to the costume contest registration desk after the parade is over, Iska."

"This is a lot of work! I feel like I'm part of the carnival's cast at this point!"

"They said they don't have enough help. Apparently, they have twelve different contests all over Bachils."

"Wow...," Iska replied.

"It's famous worldwide, after all. The Twelfth Street contest is especially well regarded. It's a contest for super-cute cosplayers!" Commander Mismis's eyes glittered brightly underneath her large black hat. "Pro models come from all over the world to enter. The judges are big shots, too, so anyone who wins gets a ticket straight into the upper crust!"

"Huh. I didn't know it was that big of a deal."

Come to think of it, Iska seemed to remember that the girls he had bumped into had said something about the Twelfth Street contest.

"A contest, huh? If Alice were participating, I bet all eyes would be on her...but she couldn't possibly be here."

He looked around. He felt a sense of apprehension, since he could have sworn he'd sensed someone like her nearby.

"She couldn't be..."

The Ice Calamity Witch Aliceliese was a Sovereignty princess.

She wouldn't wander into enemy territory, and there was no way she would enter a costume contest, either.

"Iska, we should get going to help the entry desk soon."

"Got it."

Commander Mismis signaled for him to come, and Iska left the parade.

"All right, we've made you wait long enough!

"This is the thirty-seventh Bachils city-state costume grand prix! Royalty, the entertainment industry, and artists have an eye on this contest, no matter where in the world they are!

"Who will have the honor of winning this time?!"

They were at the Twelfth Street plaza. At least a few thousand people had gathered to watch, and that was a conservative estimate. Since the whole thing was broadcast on TV, the contest was already firing up.

"I'm surprised it's this big..."

They were backstage. Alice listened to the cheers of the crowd from the waiting room for the candidates.

"They're very excited. I must say it's quite impressive, even for an ally nation of the enemy."

"Um, Lady Alice, can we talk...?" In contrast to Alice, who was in awe, Rin, the person actually entering the contest, seemed uncomfortable. "I know it's cowardly, but may I please withdraw? An average person like me won't stand a chance in this thing..."

"The competition does go far beyond what I imagined," Alice admitted.

All the contestants were stunningly gorgeous men and women.

The costumes ranged from tried-and-true witches, to werewolves, to zombies, to vampires, and more. Every single one of them seemed to shine bright, and their costumes looked authentic.

Their outfits had all been custom-made, and they even had makeup artists.

"Uh, um... Everyone else is so much taller than me and better looking... Um, Lady Alice, you might be able to compete, but someone like me..."

Alice's elegance and appearance were fit for royalty, and they would give her a fighting chance.

But Rin was just an attendant. When it came down to it, she worked behind the scenes in the shadows, so she wasn't used to being in the spotlight. Alice could understand why she was feeling uncomfortable.

"Right... I hate to admit it, but that vampire and succubus were correct. We're out of our league." She sighed and placed a gentle hand on Rin's shoulder. "Rin, you should pull out. You have your talents, and there's no point in fighting a battle that you don't need to."

"Lady Alice!"

Tears filled Rin's eyes.

A loud roar came from the spectators in the plaza outside.

"Oh? Is it starting?"

The judges had gotten onstage along with the host, who was holding a microphone.

"Allow me to introduce our guest and chief judge! We have an excellent guest, just as we do every year! Dare I say it, but I think we've outdone ourselves this time!" the host announced with excitement.

As applause rang out, an elderly man appeared onstage.

"I present to you our judge—the Empire's treasure, nay, the treasure

of the entire world. This man, who is the distillation of what an artist should be, has singlehandedly pushed the definition of beauty to its next stage! We have for you the living treasure, Master Daiban Ga Pinchi!"

"Salutations!" A man with a magnificent white beard walked onstage. He was beefy, like a pro wrestler. A sharp glint sparkled in his eyes, and as he stood there, he exuded the overpowering air of an expert martial artist.

"I'm the living treasure Daiban!" he said.

"He couldn't possibly be?!" Alice cried out without thinking as she looked up at him.

Alice wasn't the only one who'd had that reaction. Even the other famous judges onstage had widened their eyes in surprise.

"M-Master Daiban?!"

"You mean the legendary artist has left the Imperial capital?!"

"Master Daiban, I've been your fan ever since I was a kid. Please let me shake your hand!"

One of the judges, a big shot from the movie industry, froze up, and another, an actress, began to cry as they all welcomed Daiban.

Daiban, the living treasure.

The man was a legend who resided in the Empire. His work spanned every form of art, from ceramics, calligraphy, poetry, sculpture, painting, music, even to gourmet food, and he pushed every medium to its fullest extent. His name had crossed borders, earning him passionate fans from countries all over the world.

"It's Master Daiban?!"

And Alice was one of those fans, of course.

In fact, there was only a single person present who was unfamiliar with him.

"Who's that overbearing old man?"

"Rin! You don't know the master artist?! He's a treasure to the world!" Alice latched on to Rin's shoulders and shouted as her eyebrows rose up. "If I went into the Empire to destroy the capital, I would never touch Master Daiban's workshop. Not if it meant harming any of his pieces…"

"What if you did?"

"The entire world would denounce the Nebulis Sovereignty. Every nation across the globe would declare war on us!"

Even a Nebulis princess stood no chance against this old man. In other words, he lived up to his title as a living treasure.

"Ridiculous!"

"That's how important Master Daiban is!" Alice insisted.

All the other candidates backstage were looking excited.

"W-wait, it's actually Master Daiban!"

"I can't believe it. If we win, well, he's super famous!"

Even the vampire and the succubus who had picked a fight with Alice had a twinkle in their eyes.

"Huh, so I guess he's an impressive guy. But that has nothing to do with me anymore, since I'm withdrawing. Let's go, Lady Alice."

"What are you saying, Rin?"

"……Huh?"

"Master Daiban is here! You can't run now!" Alice grabbed her attendant's hand before she could leave. "You need to participate, Rin! I'm sure you can do it. You need to win and let me take a picture to commemorate this fortuitous experience with Master Daiban!"

"That's not what you said earlier!"

The costume grand prix had opened. Things kicked off with the judges' greetings.

"Please go ahead, Master Daiban!"

"All right."

The living treasure walked to the front of the stage.

"Ladies and gentlemen, what is art?!" he howled, pointing at the audience. "I am always in constant pursuit of it. Art is the battle with the universe within you! You build up both your spirit and your creativity until you create a new universe. Do you follow?"

"What? What is that old man say—?"

"Quiet, Rin."

"Mrff?!"

As Alice clamped a hand over the mouth of her attendant, the old man continued with his greeting.

"And this competition is no exception. It's a clash between souls who have pursued personal betterment of their own accord. Present to us a new age of art that will make even me gasp in amazement! Usher in a new dimension of creation!"

"Maybe we should take that geezer to the looney bin…," Rin murmured rather riskily.

On the other hand, Daiban seemed to be filled with a sense of accomplishment after his speech.

"Whew… I always feel excited talking to the youth, no matter the generation."

"Thank you so much, Master!"

The host gave him a slight bow, and behind him, applause roared out from the audience.

"Amazing…"

"Master Daiban is incredible. I feel the same happiness seeing him as when I watch a first-rate concert."

"Yeah, my ears feel like they're in heaven."

The three other judges looked like they were satisfied.

"There's definitely something wrong with this! Why were they so moved by that speech?!"

"Quit it, Rin. Stop complaining and get ready. We're about to start."

As Alice and Rin watched the stage, the candidates walked up one at a time under the gaze of the audience.

"All right! The first one looks wonderful! Please welcome Dietfriet the werewolf to the stage. He's a theater actor from a neighboring country. His handsome face and muscular build have earned him success as a magazine model. We already have one amazing candidate for the grand prix onstage!"

The crowd didn't hold back their applause. The cheers of the younger women were particularly impressive, even drowning out the host's voice.

"This is too much, Lady Alice. There's an actual actor out there!"

"Yes. The audience is really responsive, so you need to get great results, too."

Dietfriet had found the perfect contrast by pairing his handsome good looks with the horrific image of a werewolf. He was also bare-chested, and his muscular physique was a staggering sight.

"That body paint subbing in for fur on his muscles really works. It shows how powerful a werewolf is. A mummy girl who's just wrapped bandages around herself will have some tough competition," Alice commented.

"This isn't even a competition if it's plain impossible for me to put up a fight! How can you think I have a chance against him?!"

"Shh. Rin, the judging is about to begin."

The murmuring crowd quieted.

"First, we'll have the three judges give their scores!

"We'll hear from the playwright Michael, the composer Nasrivon, and the winner of the best international actress award, Flamie.

"They may award each contestant up to ten points. The total points anyone can receive is thirty. Judges, if you please!"

The judges gave seven, six, and eight points, for a total of twenty-one.

The moment the judges' scores showed up on a board, a large cheer filled the area.

"And there you have it, a twenty-one!

"That's an average of seven from our discerning judges. Last year's winner had a total of twenty-four, so this is actually a pretty high score!"

Even Dietfriet looked pleased and nodded from the stage.

However…

The true judging would only begin now.

Only those who received a fifteen or higher from the first three judges could move on for a judgment from Daiban.

"Rin, listen closely. Based on my quick research, the next judgment isn't based on points."

"What do you mean?"

"It's all or nothing. If Master Daiban raises his flag, then you go on to the second judgment round. If you don't, then you're dropped out on the spot."

"That sounds harsh…"

"Yes. That's why it's a nerve-racking moment."

It was quiet again.

"All right, Master Daiban, please give your evaluation."

The elderly man sat in his special seat. As the spectators looked on in anticipation, Daiban crossed his arms and didn't so much as move an inch.

He didn't even make a move to pick up his flag.

"Oh my…looks like Dietfriet didn't make it, folks! The flag is still down. Master Daiban has blocked him!"

Evidently, Daiban wasn't going to compromise. If he didn't like what he saw, he wouldn't even give the person praise or empty commendation. He was the type of man to mercilessly incinerate his own artwork if it didn't meet his standards.

Hence he was known as the Artist of Fire.

"S-so, the next candidate is the fairy Bridgit! I'm sure this young acting prodigy needs no introduction!"

No one could deny she was cute. Even Alice thought she looked like a beautiful fairy straight from a fable.

"All right, let's get the three judges' scores. Oh! Looks like we've got a twenty. Now that's a good score, like our first candidate!"

But the audience wasn't cheering nearly as much. Everyone there had already realized something: The true trial came after the judges gave their scores.

"A-all right, Master Daiban."

"…It's all wrong." The artist kept his arms crossed. "She doesn't have the beauty I'm after, either. Better luck next time."

"Looks like that wasn't a pass, either! It seems she hasn't measured up to Master Daiban's eyes, just the same as the first candidate!"

Alice didn't understand what was going on. She couldn't see how the costumes could be improved, so why did Daiban look so sullen?

"Uh, um, Master Daiban, so why did the last candidate not pass muster…?"

"Who do you think I am?" The elderly man's eyes opened wide as he glared at the host. "Compared to the princess of Mien from the beautiful and faraway country to the east, that girl's fairy costume isn't even cute."

"I—I see. So you've met the legendary princess, then?!"

"Not only that, but the only one who could compare in feminine charm is the Nebulis Sovereignty's First Princess Elletear. No one can measure up to her beauty."

"Oh, oh my…!"

"Isn't charm and charisma the equivalent of art?" The old man's words echoed firmly throughout the place. "Bridgit is cute, and yes, her costume looks authentic. But just because she can attract attention doesn't mean she can move people's hearts. What I seek is something that will breathe new life into the arts and shake up the world!"

"I-I'm terribly sorry! Of course, Master Daiban!"

The other candidates backstage looked grim as they listened to the man's passionate reasoning. No wonder he was a great artist and a living legend. Just because someone was conventionally attractive didn't guarantee they could sway him with their looks.

"You see, candidates! You need to challenge yourself to create a new universe that will make me burn with creativity!"

The evaluations continued, going through the third candidate, then the fourth, and the fifth, all beautiful men and women whose features were enhanced by their equally gorgeous makeup.

"No! Wrong, all wrong!" Daiban angrily shouted. "This isn't even close to the art I want to see!"

"Which means...?"

"Another rejection!"

"Wh-what a difficult grand prix we're having this year, folks!"

The host gulped.

"So we've gotten through half of the hundred candidates and have zero who have moved on to the second round. This competition seems to have the highest barriers for progression we've ever had!"

They were in the second half of the judging, but Daiban had yet to uncross his arms.

Then they finally reached the ninety-ninth contestant.

"Lady Alice! Those two women are going up! The vampire and succubus who picked a fight with us in the changing room!"

"Oh! Now these two ladies here!" the host said.

The audience suddenly grew excited.

A blond vampire and a black-haired succubus came up as a pair.

"There they are! The pride of Bachils! Our young charismatic models Hiellen and Caldelia. They're the favorites tonight!"

The vampire was both frightening and beautiful. The succubus was captivating. Their reputation was well-earned. They had the charm to captivate anyone who saw them. Even the women in the audience could see that beauty was right in front of them.

"All right! We'll get the three judges' scores! Nine, nine, and ten!"

The total was twenty-eight. Their high marks were undisputed.

"And what does Master Daiban think? Of course these young women would...sir?"

The entire stage went silent.

The main judge, Daiban, didn't make a move. When he showed no sign of picking up his flag, the host and the other judges seemed surprised.

"W-wait a second!"

"We've been watching the whole time, and we're the last ones!"

The succubus and the vampire were both shouting.

The two women walked past the host and came right up to Daiban's special seat.

"What do you think you're doing, old man?! You can't behave like this just because you're a famous artist."

"You're putting on airs. I bet you're just jealous of young talent like us."

"..." Daiban said nothing to them.

"H-hey! Answer us!"

"You brats." He finally did as they asked.

"Urgh?!"

The glint in his eyes pierced them as sharply as a knife. They backed away.

"Which part of the stage were you looking at?" he asked.

"……Huh?"

"The two of you didn't even look at the audience once you got onto the stage. You only stared at me the whole time. Isn't that right?"

"Uhh?!"

"W-well…!"

It was as though he'd recited a holy incantation. The succubus and the vampire staggered when Daiban said this, like they'd been hit with purifying light.

"Why are you dressing up, and who is this carnival for? And where is your gratitude for the people who came to cheer you on?"

Thousands were behind Daiban to support them, but the two young women hadn't even given the audience a passing glance.

"The true star of the show isn't me, it's the thousands of spectators gathered here. Don't you think you've lost sight of what the true spirit of this carnival is?"

"…Urgh. Ah…"

"Y-you're right…"

The pair fell to their knees.

"How could we forget something so fundamental…?"

"I can't believe we were so caught up by our status that we forgot to be grateful and overlooked the true spirit of the carnival."

"However!" The old man rose to his feet. Then he grabbed the two ladies' hands and forced them up. "There are infinite possibilities within you. You must remain strong. Stand and pursue the right path of the arts from here on."

"I'm so sorry, Master Daiban!"

"We see the error of our ways!"

The two women hugged the man. He was like a stubborn old grandfather reconciling with his granddaughters in a heartwarming scene.

"Splendid!"

"That's what makes him Master Daiban!"

"Yeah, he saved the two women from drowning in talent and brought them right back. What a beautiful ending to a superb show!"

The judges were all crying.

Even the audience gave them a generous applause.

The mellow atmosphere led right into the conclusion of the contest.

"How moving! This is all so moving! We had no winners, but I'm sure the thirty-seventh grand prix will live on as a legend.

"All right, everyone, see you next—"

"Please wait!" Alice shouted, dispelling the festive atmosphere. "You still have one more candidate left! My attendant, Rin!"

"Lady Alice, please don't! They were just about to forget me and finish it, and you ruined it!"

"C'mon, just go up!"

"Ahh?!"

Alice pushed Rin onto the stage.

"Oh, I'm sorry! Looks like we had one more contestant all along! So, mummy girl, I'm handing it off to you to introduce yourself!"

"I-I'm Rin, the mummy girl..."

Her face was bright red.

She managed to squeeze out an introduction, but it sounded as though it would taper off at any moment.

"I—I can't believe someone like me is on a stage like this...and wearing this outfit. It's humiliating..."

Rin had never been in front of an audience of several thousand before—and to make matters worse, she was dressed in nothing but bandages.

"You can do it, Rin! Just get over your distress, and glory will be yours for the taking!"

"But I don't want glory like that!" She was so mortified that her face turned an even brighter shade of red when Alice cheered her on.

"All right, Rin! Sell yourself!"

"Y-yes..."

They had a minute to introduce themselves.

A succubus would give the audience a sexy pose, and a werewolf would try to howl to show his ferocity. That was generally what people did.

However...

Rin couldn't even attempt anything nearly as daring as that. As someone who had dedicated herself to becoming a guard and to martial arts, she had no tricks up her sleeve to help her on a stage.

What could she do?

"Th-the only thing I can do...is a little martial arts."

"Oh? Now that's an interesting party trick. It seems very practical."

"Th-then I'll show off my technique with a dagger..."

She unwrapped the bandage on her right hand and to reveal a hidden knife. Even dressed as a mummy, she'd made sure to keep a weapon on her person.

It took only a moment.

The audience hadn't even been able to tell when she had pulled out the dagger.

"Huh? When did you get a knife?"

"Th-then I'll start. Ugh! Desperate times call for desperate measures!" she yelled, red in the face.

As she held her knife, she fluttered through the air.

She was quick.

Rather than those of a ballerina or dancer charismatically flitting through the air, her movements exhibited the strength of a goat leaping through rocky terrain.

"Uh, so this is unexpected..." The host looked dumbfounded. *"W-wow. This is amazing...but, um, Miss Mummy? You do realize this is a costume contest, don't you?"*

Though Rin's display showed off her physical prowess, it wasn't what the judges were looking for.

"Uh, umm."

"Th-this is the only thing I can do, though!"

She spun through the air.

Rin landed with enough beauty to put a gymnast to shame. The show had all worked out fine until that point, but Rin had forgotten about the force that went into doing a full rotation. Along with the fact that she was dressed only in bandages instead of her usual outfit.

"Oh......"

Swish... Her costume started to unravel.

Her slender torso and stomach were laid bare. Then even the bandages around her armpits and neck fell to the floor.

"Nooooo!"

She was very nearly naked.

Rin quickly tried to hide her chest, but the entire audience had already gotten a good look at her bare skin.

"N-no one wants to see my skinny little body!"

"What an unexpected incident! Looks like we can't go on. Unfortunately, we'll need to disquali—"

"Waaaaait!"

The host's announcement was interrupted by a roar from the special guest.

"This girl isn't just anyone!"

"...Huh? Master Daiban?"

The audience and judges stirred.

The previously unmoving artist had finally risen from his seat.

"Let us carefully observe the mummy girl!" he said.

Rin sat on the floor, seeming mortified as the audience's eyes focused on her.

"Mummies hide themselves under bandages, yet this mummy girl has removed hers on her own. How original! Rin, or whatever your name is, this is the aesthetic I was looking for!"

"But it was just an accident!"

"No, it's an emergence. Just as a butterfly breaks through its chrysalis after metamorphosis, the mummy girl removes her bandages to discover herself. That must be it!"

"N-no, I wasn't trying to—"

"How spectacular! What a finely calculated performance!"

"Listen to meee!"

Daiban disregarded Rin's protests.

"And also—" Daiban was staring straight at Rin, who was almost totally naked. "—take a close look at her without her bandages."

"Please don't!" she cried.

"Gaze upon her beautiful physique. She's not just anyone!" Daiban, who was well acquainted with the human form, opened his eyes wide. "Every bit of her body has a use. She has no fat, which means she has no waste."

"I'm so sorry for barely having breasts, okay!"

"And her physique wasn't artificially created through going to the gym. Her body is like that of a lion. Like a beast striding through the wilderness!"

Daiban was actually right. Rin had originally trained her body for martial arts, so she wasn't built like an actress or a model.

"What a frightening girl you are. Once you abandoned your bandages, you revealed a body of steel. That is the mummy girl's transformation. I'm astounded!"

"Okay, that's really enough..."

"This was truly the costume marking a new age of art that I was looking for!" Daiban yelled.

"Master Daiban. In other words, do you mean Rin the mummy girl is...?"

"In my eyes, she isn't lacking in a single area!"

Daiban pulled out a folding fan and held it over Rin's head. The word *Bravo!* was written across it in his own handwriting.

"She is most certainly the winner!"

There was a great cheer. The entire audience and the judges all gave her a standing ovation. Not a single person was in their seats.

And in the midst of this moment of triumph...

"I don't get it..."

Only Rin herself seemed dissatisfied.

Rin had won.

At the very end of the show, all the participants took a photo together. Alice placed herself right next to Daiban and was quite pleased.

"Rin, that was superb! Even I was proud of how you handled that!"

"Th-thank you, Lady Alice. I'm afraid I can't say that I share the same sentiment..."

"Chin up, Rin! Be proud!"

The commemorative photo also happened to have the two mascots, Bowell and Rabi, in it as well. They were both wearing large costumes, so Alice had assumed that men were inside them.

"Hey, Iska, move to the right more."

"I just can't see anything. Jhin, you get closer instead."

They were whispering to each other, so Alice couldn't make out most of what they said.

"Ahh…because I won, I got hit with a ton of interviews and lost all that time. We didn't even have enough time to gather intel on the enemy state…"

"But you know what, Rin? I was satisfied with everything you did."

Yes. Alice didn't have any complaints about this trip.

But if she could say one very small thing that she would have liked…

"I wish Iska had been here so we could have had a costume showdown. Oh well."

"Lady Alice, did you say something?"

"No, nothing."

She wondered what kind of costume he would wear if he had been here.

As she pondered that, Alice took the picture with the mascots who were directly behind her.

File 04

Our Last Crusade or the Undefeatable Big Sister

Our Last CRUSADE OR THE RISE OF A New World
Secret File

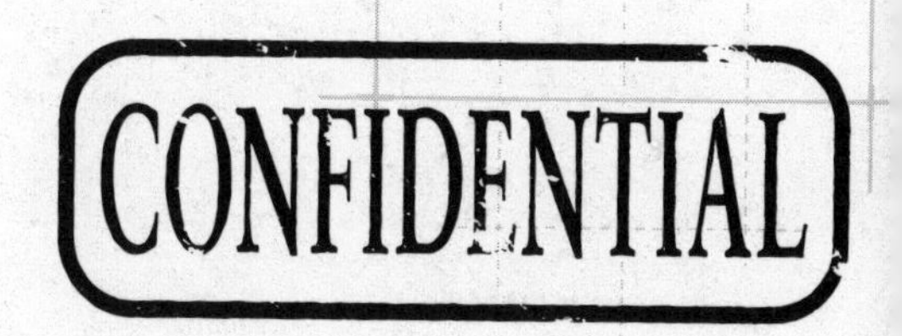

1

The witch's paradise—aka the Nebulis Sovereignty—was a nation of people who possessed supernatural energy called astral power.

One day in the royal palace...

"Yes, I'm enjoying this brush!" Alice yelled with vigor, a paintbrush in her hand.

Aliceliese Lou Nebulis IX.

Her brilliant golden hair and charming face were her most striking features. The enemy Imperial forces were terrified of her and had dubbed her the Ice Calamity Witch, but in her regular life, the moniker hardly suited her.

At the moment, Alice was...

"Oh! Aha!"

...passionately wielding a paintbrush.

However, she wasn't painting so much as pummeling the canvas, as though the brush were her weapon.

"Sir, how is this?!" she exclaimed.

"Oh? You seem to be even more enthusiastic with your brushes today than normal, Princess Alice."

A court painter stroked his beard as he approached her. He was her art instructor.

This was a painting lesson, which was fitting for a princess, as she needed to be cultured.

Yet a moment later, Alice stopped in her tracks. She was no longer flailing her brush around.

"How odd..."

She raised her head. Her eyes met a houseplant, which was presumably her subject.

"Sir, I have a question about something I don't understand."

"What is it, Princess Alice?"

"I'm motivated, and I have a zeal for using my paintbrush, and I'm even working under the instruction of a court painter. These should be the perfect conditions to paint."

"Yes, you're quite right."

"But this piece of mine..."

Her canvas looked nothing like the plant she was trying to paint.

Instead, she had depicted something resembling an eldritch horror crawling over a table using its green tentacles. It was straight from a horror movie.

......*Why does it look like this?*

Alice was sure she had been painting a houseplant showered in radiant sunlight.

"Oh? Oh my!" However, her instructor seemed to be genuinely ecstatic when he glanced at her work. "Princess Alice, you've improved yet again! Look at this novel and unique use of color and brushstrokes. You've completely deconstructed the original shape of the houseplant so that it's unrecognizable...now this is creative. No layperson could hope to express such artistic talent!"

Alice, however, remained silent.

"Oh, what is it, Lady Alice?"

"I feel so very conflicted..."

Though Alice appreciated the compliments for her creativity, she had wanted to create a more naturalistic painting.

"Sir, I was trying to...take a more photorealistic approach with this piece."

"Hmm. I believe that the best path forward would be to nurture your creative tendencies, Lady Alice."

The man cleared his throat. "All right. Well, if I am to provide some concrete advice, let us start with this grotesque tentacle here—"

"That's the plant."

"Oh, pardon me. Now, Lady Alice, the way to obtain photorealistic quality to your art is to focus on shadow. For example...the shadow of a houseplant would take dark green with a touch of blue blended in. Then the areas where the sun strikes the leaf would require a bit of yellow—"

The instructor launched into an impassioned lecture.

But was that all true? If she just gave it some shadows and adjusted the colors, would this tentacle monster really start to look like a houseplant? She felt like something was off about her piece on an even more fundamental level. It was like she was entirely missing some quality that was indispensable to painting.

"This really isn't going well for me. Oh, right. How are you doing, Sisbell?"

She remembered that her little sister was with her and turned to face her.

A total of two students were attending the art lesson. Alice, the Sovereignty's second princess, was one of them. The other was the third princess, Sisbell. Her little sister was also currently practicing. Unlike Alice, she was incredibly quiet and was only dabbing her paintbrush.

But how was her canvas looking?

Alice wanted to see.

"Sisbell, how is your painting? Is it progressing along?" she asked nonchalantly.

She would just take a tiny peek. The moment she stole a glance, however...

"What is this?!" She was absolutely shocked. Alice's eyes went wide when she saw her little sister's work. "S-Sisbell, this painting is..."

"Hmm. This really isn't going well for me. I haven't tried my hand at art in some time, and I'm afraid I'm out of practice. Oh? What is it, dear sister?"

Her sister turned to her.

Sisbell Lou Nebulis.

She had striking strawberry blond hair and charming features. Because her features still had a girlish quality, she looked adorable, almost doll-like.

"Oh, you were asking about my painting? I'm embarrassed to say that it's been so long that I've become terrible at painting."

"Terribly good, you mean..."

"What?"

"Oh, uh, nothing!" Alice quickly lost all nerve to look at her sister's canvas and turned away.

......*What is with that?!*

......*She's way too good at this!*

Sisbell had perfectly captured the vivacious green of the

houseplant and the faintly warm sunlight filtering through the curtains. It was a perfectly traditional painting.

By comparison, Alice's was a garish collection of tentacles.

"Hmm... You're pretty good, Sisbell, I must say. Yes, quite passable. It looks like the instructor really helped you."

"So how is your painting then, Alice?"

"What?"

She froze. When her little sister looked at her with curiosity, Alice backed away.

"You saw my painting, so I'd like to see yours as well."

"What? I-I'm still working on it. It's...a draft."

"Then I'd like a peek."

"N-no, Sisbell! It's still—"

Before Alice could stop her, Sisbell picked up the canvas.

She stared hard enough to bore holes through the painting. And then...

"Pfft..."

"Did you just laugh?! You just laughed, didn't you?!"

"Of course not. I was just so deeply moved... Hee-hee. Pfft!"

As she said that, Sisbell didn't even bother to hide her pitying smile.

"Good gracious...it's quite a piece of work, though. Now, what are these green tentacles here? They're quite grotesque and eerie to look at. In fact, they look slightly obscene."

"Obscene?!"

"You don't mean to tell me these are meant to be the plant's leaves? I'm so very jealous of your originality."

"Grrrr?!"

She had made a big miscalculation. Alice hadn't thought her sister would be so good at traditional painting.

"Uh, um, if I may, Princess Alice and Princess Sisbell? I think it's wonderful you each have your own styles—" As the instructor tried to mediate, Alice cut him off and pointed at her sister.

"I challenge you to a battle, Sisbell! If you think you can look down on me just because of a single canvas, you've made a huge mistake!"

"So what would you like to do?"

"I haven't shown you what I'm truly capable of. And it seems that you still need an education in culture and art befitting a true princess."

"A true princess? Ha-ha! Are you saying that you are a true princess, Alice?" Sisbell was confident. The slight girl proudly thrust out her chest. "Yes, you do have something amazing, Alice. I don't have the strong astral powers you do, so I can't fight on a battlefield, and I am somewhat jealous of your shamelessly well-developed bust, but—"

"What about my bust is shameless?!"

"However! When it comes to being a princess, you cannot beat me in anything. I, the Third Princess Sisbell, have the true qualities befitting a princess!"

"Well, now you've said it."

As she hid her canvas behind her, Alice faced her sister head-on.

Her little sister was actually cute. She was as sweet as a kitten. Even her mischievous smile had its charms.

But none of that mattered now that she had challenged her.

"It's a duel, Sisbell! With our pride as princesses at stake!"

"A battle to show who is the true princess! That's exactly what I needed."

"I'll show you that no little sister can surpass her big sister!" Alice declared.

"Hee-hee. But there's one right here who has."

Sparks flew between the two siblings.

But just as the battle between the second and the third daughters began, there was a light knock at the door.

"Alice, Sisbell, are you in here?" A clear voice was followed by a woman of incomparable beauty. The most striking aspects about her were her lustrous emerald hair and her bosom, which was even larger than Alice's.

"Elletear?!"

"Sister, what are you doing here?!"

Alice and Sisbell both shouted in surprise simultaneously.

"It's been quite some time. I'm glad to see you're doing well." The woman smiled.

Elletear Lou Nebulis. She was the first princess—in other words, the oldest daughter making up the trio of sisters.

"S-Sister…!" Sisbell faltered. After the big show she had put on for Alice, she looked intimidated. "Sister, I thought that you were campaigning overseas…"

"I'm finished with that, so I've come home. I heard you were here in the art room, so I thought I would visit you."

She smiled, then she shifted her attention to the instructor behind them.

"Well, if it isn't Michelandaro the painter."

"Y-you know my name?!"

"Of course I do."

"It is an honor. You look ever more beautiful, Lady Elletear!"

"Ha-ha, you're too kind."

Charmed by Elletear's looks, the painter turned into a fawning mess. Yes, this was their older sister, Elletear. Within the Sovereignty, she had looks that were rumored to rival a goddess's, and it was said she could easily make any man fall for her. Alice and Sisbell simply couldn't compare.

"So, Alice, Sisbell." Elletear turned to face them. "You were shouting earlier. It doesn't do well to fight."

"We weren't fighting," Sisbell replied instantly. "We're staking our pride on a duel. It's a very noble venture."

"And how will you go about doing that?"

"We will be competing to see who is the better princess."

"Hee-hee…" In that moment, there was something ominous about Elletear's graceful laugh. "Well, that sounds fun."

"Elletear?"

"All right then." She clapped her hands and beamed as she declared, "Then how about I participate?"

"What?!"

"W-wait, sister!"

Neither Alice nor Sisbell could believe her ears. Hold on. This wasn't good. A formidable opponent had just entered the arena.

"Please wait, Elletear! This was a personal duel between Alice and me… So, um…"

"Sisbell? You really should share the fun," Elletear smoothly dismissed her. "Oh, I know. We can ask the ministers to be the judges and have the queen and our people spectate."

"B-but, Elletear!"

"Sisbell." A glint flashed in Elletear's eyes. "Didn't you just say that you have the qualities of a true princess? I believe that's what I heard."

"You were listening to us?!"

They had touched on her pride as the eldest. Forget letting sleeping dogs lie—they'd prodded a dragon awake. By the time they realized it, it was already too late.

"I—I was just saying it because of what Alice said first…"

"Sisbell! Don't put the blame on me!"

"Well, I'm looking forward to this," Elletear cheerfully continued as Alice and Sisbell panicked.

And thus started the very first True Princess Competition between the three sisters.

The night before the competition, Alice prepared for the battle in which her pride as a princess was on the line.

"It's time for a strategy session!" Alice called Rin into her room. "Ever since we decided to do the competition, I've been working on being more dignified as a princess, but I'm far from prepared..."

Alice also needed to stay on top of her duties as a candidate for queen. In other words, she was incredibly busy. She had to attend important meetings and greet special guests from overseas.

"I didn't have much time..."

She had worked as hard as she could to cultivate herself and refine her dignity as a princess in the spare moments she'd had.

Her sisters must have done the same, though. She'd received reports that both Elletear and Sisbell had been hard at work as well.

"Rin, please be honest." She stared into her attendant's eyes and nodded. "How likely is it that you think I'll win tomorrow?"

"That you'll win?"

"Yes. And don't spare my feelings. I want to know what you truly think."

"I would say 0.02 percent," Rin replied.

"That's a bit too honest, don't you think?!" She slapped her desk and stood up. "It's the night before the competition. The person you serve is nervous, so you could have at least said 40 percent or 50!"

"You said not to spare your feelings, Lady Alice."

"I—I suppose I did..."

The competition was between three people, which meant they each had a one-in-three shot of winning in a vacuum, so Alice had been hoping Rin would say that at least.

"So, Rin, how did you arrive at that number?"

"Sisbell has a 40 percent chance of winning. Based on the themes covered tomorrow, I think it could even be 50-50."

"Then why..."

"Because of Lady Elletear," Rin declared. "Yes, you're a wonderful princess, Lady Alice, but her incredible beauty and noble dignity make her incomparable to any other person in the Sovereignty's history."

"Urgh?!"

"Now we just wait for the day of. We can only hope that Elletear withdraws due to a stomachache."

"Then you think it's hopeless?!"

"Yes. That's why I put your odds at 0.02 percent."

"Rin, you dummy!"

And so their strategy session wasn't very useful.

......No, actually...

......I already knew.

No little sister could surpass her big sister. Elletear was basically a living testament to that. She was more prim and proper than anyone in the Sovereignty, and more beautiful, too, not to mention cultured.

Alice knew she was up against frightful competition. If they had been duking it out on the battlefield, Alice would have won as the strongest princess in the Sovereignty, but she had few prospects of that being one of the themes for the next day's competition.

"What should I do...?"

Ding ding. Right at that moment in the middle of the night, the bell to Alice's room rang.

"Excuse me...," came a voice.

"Sisbell?!"

Alice doubted her eyes when her little sister entered the room. They would be enemies the next day, so she could only wonder why Sisbell was visiting her room so late into the night.

"What's wrong, Sisbell?"

"I wanted to talk to you about something, Alice..." Sisbell closed the door. Then she looked at Rin as well. "I see. So you were having a strategy session together to prepare for tomorrow's competition."

"Huh?! Th-that's top secret!"

"You don't need to hide it from me. In fact, that's what I wanted to talk to you about."

"And what's that?"

"I'll get straight to the point." Sisbell took in a deep breath. "Let's join forces."

"......Huh?"

"You already sense it, too, don't you? We have no chance of winning against Elletear in tomorrow's fight."

"Huh?!"

"We miscalculated. I can't believe she came home earlier than we anticipated..." Sisbell balled her hands into fists. She sounded like a real tactician, what with the way she was speaking as though her sister were the enemy. "I hate to admit it, but Elletear is the most beautiful person in the Sovereignty. She has looks and brains, and she's also graceful and charming. We might as well call her the most perfect big sister in the world... Unlike my second sister."

"What did you just say?"

"Never mind. Anyway, if we take on this challenge separately, we have no chance."

"...Yes, you're right." Alice reluctantly nodded. "But wait,

Sisbell, we're supposed to fight each other tomorrow. If the two of us team up, wouldn't that be against the rules?"

"Rest assured that I have no intention of breaking the rules. We'll pick off Elletear first. That's all I'm proposing."

They would make Elletear drop out of the competition first. After that, the two of them could have their face-off. Then only a single victor would emerge.

"It was originally a match between the two of us. Elletear just forced her way into it."

"You have a point..."

They had no time to hesitate. The day of the competition was already approaching.

"Sisbell." Alice held out her right hand. "Let's fight our invincible sister together!"

"Yes!"

And so the second and the third sisters gave each other a firm handshake during their clandestine meeting in the middle of the night.

2

It was the day of the competition.

As Alice and Sisbell entered the meeting hall, they were met with an ardent crowd that couldn't fit into the provided seating.

"We have all our competitors!"

The defense minister was acting as the host. Though he normally scowled during meetings, today he seemed excited for what was to come.

"We have gathered here today three of the most charming

sisters around, each claiming that she is the true princess. And now they'll compete against each other, with their pride on the line!"

"*Woooo!*"

The audience gave them a thunderous round of applause and cheered, shaking the hall.

"They're really watching us..."

"Hah! Why, of course." As the audience called her name, Sisbell responded with a charming smile. She didn't seem too displeased by the attention. "I rarely am in front of people, but if they have such high expectations of me, that changes things. I'll show them my princess powers."

"Princess powers?"

"Yes. That's a quantitative measure of a princess's grace. Say we measured earlier, and you were a nine—then I would have been a two hundred," Sisbell said.

"That hardly seems fair!"

"No, it's not. Besides, it's Elletear's princess power we really need to worry about here. And that's...huh?"

Sisbell was taken aback. She blinked. Actually, where was their older sister? She should have been there by now.

"That's odd. I wonder where Elletear is."

"She's over there, Alice!"

Sisbell pointed at a section of the audience where a particularly large group of people had gathered. In the middle of the crowd, Elletear was giving out cookies from a heaping pile in a basket she held.

"Good morning, everyone. These are my homemade cookies. Please try one."

"Wh-what?!"

Alice got a sinking feeling. Oh no.

Their sister must have gotten here earlier to hand out treats. Her cookies even had her name written out on them in chocolate. That would make her a crowd favorite for sure.

"This is bad, Sisbell. At this rate, the entire audience will be on Elletear's side!"

"Urgh! So that's what it's come to!"

Sisbell gritted her teeth in frustration. The battle had already begun.

"Elletear, that's as far as you'll go pulling your tricks!"

"Oh, Alice, Sisbell, good morning."

Their sister was calm and composed as she turned around. She had pleasant smile on her face, but that was undoubtedly for the sake of the audience.

"This is the decisive battle." Sisbell looked up at her older sister. "Prepare yourself for what's to come! I'll make you fold today, Elletear!"

"Oh, Sisbell, you're coming on quite strong. But I'm confident about my chances. Don't you think I should be, Defense Minister?"

"Indeed!" The minister grabbed his mic again. "The first annual True Princess Competition is a three-game match. In other words, you'll compete in three subject areas to receive a score quantifying your princessliness! And it seems that Princess Elletear has a decisive lead in winning over the audience!"

"And there you have it," Elletear added.

She laughed and gave Sisbell a mature smile.

"I think you could even try to team up against me, if you'd like."

Neither Alice nor Sisbell replied.

"I am the eldest, after all. You can have that as a freebie."

"Hah... Don't push your luck!" Sisbell pointed at her.

"I was waiting for you to say that. Then Alice and I will tag team, just as you suggested!"

"What?!"

The audience started to shout in excitement.

"What unexpected circumstances. It seems the two princesses have decided to join forces!"

"Making light of someone will simply lead to your own downfall. You would never take back your words, though—especially as a princess—right?"

"Why, I would never," Elletear answered with a smile.

Even though it was now two against one, she seemed to be enjoying herself.

"You won't be relaxed for long. We will beat you." Sisbell pointed at Elletear. "This is no longer three princesses against each other. In other words, it's our ultimate perfect big sister against the incompetent second sister and the lovely little sister!"

"Who are you calling incompetent?!" Alice said.

Maybe she'd have been better off aligning herself with Elletear. As the thought crossed Alice's mind, a bugle rang out.

"We are beginning the match!" the host shouted. "There are three competitions to prove who's got what it takes to be a princess. We'll kick things off with battle number one! The princesses will engage in a duel of culture, as befitting their positions!"

"Culture! That works for me. I was expecting it." Alice nodded as she saw what was displayed on the monitors.

Now, what made one a graceful princess? First and foremost was intelligence, as she would need to participate in politics. She would require a knowledge of culture as well.

......*That's why I've been reading.*

......*I've already trained for this with Rin!*

Alice and Rin had been reading history and philosophy books before going to bed every night. She was confident in the breadth of her knowledge.

"This will be in a quiz format. We will use questions relevant to the Sovereignty's culture. If you know the answer, press the button."

"Sisbell, how confident are you about this?"

"Hee-hee. Who do you think you're talking to, Alice?" Sisbell clenched her hands into fists. Yes. She was more confident than anyone here. "I'm always in my room, and I've spent half my life reading books. I'll show you how much I know!"

"So it's a quiz format? That's not good..." On the other hand, the moment she saw the topic, Elletear sighed. "I was hoping for something written, like a test. I'm so clumsy that I wonder if I'll manage to press the button."

She wasn't acting. She really looked like she had been put on the spot.

"Sisbell, we might be able to manage this!"

"Yes, don't hold back then, Alice!"

It was oldest sister versus second and third sisters.

As the audience watched, the defense minister read off the quiz question.

"First is a question about the industry in our country. The jewel of the Sovereignty that you can't go without for events and decorations..."

Ding!

Sisbell had leaned forward and pressed the button.

"Yes! The jewel that represents the Sovereignty is a blue sapphire."

"Incorrect!"

"What?!"

"The full question is, the blue sapphire is representative of the Sovereignty, but which state has gathered the most of it?"

"Oh no!" Sisbell turned pale. "I was so excited that I didn't listen to the question and sabotaged myself..."

"What are you doing, Sisbell?!"

Alice could understand how she felt.

Part of the psychology of doing quizzes like these was that everyone wanted to press the button as quickly as possible.

"Because of the incorrect answer, Princess Sisbell must wait ten seconds before answering another question."

"Alice!" Sisbell howled from next to her. "Hurry! You need to press the button before Elletear!"

"G-got it!"

Ding!

Ding!

"Oh, now that seemed simultaneous. Maybe Princess Alice was just slightly faster?"

"Oh, that's too bad." Elletear only seemed disappointed, but Alice felt like she had just barely escaped the maws of death.

"Princess Alice, what is your answer?!"

"Th-the answer is Hessen."

"________"

"Huh?"

The entire place went quiet.

Had she gotten it wrong? She felt like maybe the sixth state might have been right. Alice felt herself breaking into a cold sweat.

"Correct!"

"*Woooo!*"

The audience gave her explosive applause.

"I—I did it! I was right!"

"That's extraordinary!" Sisbell also stood up triumphantly. "Even an incompetent princess like you has your uses, I suppose!"

"Did you say something?"

"This is it, Alice! Keep it going!"

The quiz was three questions long.

They had gotten the first question right. If they could earn one more, the culture portion was theirs.

"All right, second question. But the last one was just a warmup. The next one will be much harder. Are you ready?!"

"Yes."

"I'm confident I can do this!"

"Right... I wonder if I'll be able to press the button fast enough."

The host picked up his mic again and faced the three sisters.

"Quiz question two! The question will be about a Sovereignty event. What was the name of the kitten who won in the Kitty Derby this year in Lisbahten?"

"That's impossible!"

"What kind of person would come up with a question like that?!"

Ding!

As two of the sisters protested, the third pressed the button.

"Oh, good. I finally made it. I didn't know what to do if you kept on going like last time."

Elletear sighed and dramatically wiped her forehead.

"This year's winner was a savannah Siamese named Yamada."

"Correct! Great job, First Princess. You truly are well-versed in current events!"

Wooo!

The crowd applauded just like it had for Alice—actually, even louder.

"Sisbell! Didn't you say you'd be great at this?!"

"I—I thought you said that, too, Alice!"

They both started to panic. They couldn't compete.

"Okay, Sisbell, we need to get the next one!"

"I'll give it my all, of course."

The two girls had seen just how frightening Elletear was. Their sister had outdone them in the culture section, a topic they had both thought they were well versed in.

"So in order to win..."

"Wc havc to prcss thc button before her!"

If they couldn't beat her in knowledge, they'd need to do it in speed.

They had two people. At least one of them would be able to outpace Elletear.

"And this is the last question. In the Sovereignty, the minister with the longest name—"

Ding!

Neither Alice nor Sisbell had pressed the button this time.

"What?"

"I-it can't be?!"

Alice, Sisbell, and everyone in the audience stared at Elletear. She had pressed the button before they had even finished.

"Oh my. Elletear has buzzed in. But we haven't finished the question. Are you sure about this? Are you really that confident, First Princess?!"

"Of course..."

Elletear placed a hand against her cheek and looked into the air as though she was thinking about something.

"I believe the prime minister with the longest name is Diego Jose Francisco de Paula von Nepomuceno Maria de Ros Remedios Crispin."

Hee-hee. Elletear smiled mischievously like an imp as she continued, "I think the question might be, 'What is the minister with the longest name's favorite book?' Is that right? In that case, the answer is *Love Maiden of the Light Love*."

"Correct! Amazing!"

She received thunderous applause.

Everyone in the audience rose to their feet and gave her a standing ovation.

On the other hand...

"Impossible?!"

"That's cheating! Even someone as smart as Elletear would have no way of knowing the question before it was read out fully!"

Alice and Sisbell disputed the result.

"I think we should redo this match so it's fair!"

"No, you two." Elletear turned to them. "I knew what the answer was when the quiz question was read out."

She gracefully pointed at the wall of the hall.

"Minister Diego (etc., etc., etc.)'s favorite book is over there."

"......Huh?"

"Where?"

When Alice and Sisbell looked up at the wall, they swallowed.

Portraits lined the hall, and among them were paintings of the ministers who had made significant contributions to the royal family. One of these officials was holding a book in his portrait.

"What?!"

"N-no way!"

The answer had been in the hallway this entire time.

They'd completely missed it.

"Listen, you two. The quiz may have seemed impossible, but..." Elletear raised her arms and looked at the audience. "Anyone who cares for this palace and walks around it on a day-to-day basis would notice that portrait. That's how I was able to tell what the question would be."

"Urgh?!"

"...B-but..."

"Now, as for the second question..."

As her sisters winced, Elletear continued, "You two might not remember Yamada's name, but she was actually invited to the palace to commemorate her win."

"What?"

"R-really?"

"Yes. She had her picture taken with the queen, which was published in the newspaper."

The two younger sisters had been clueless about the Kitty Derby, but evidently, Elletear had been keeping an eye on the news.

"A princess cannot learn culture simply from books. You must keep an eye on current events in the Sovereignty. Has that helped?"

She gave them a cute wink. She hadn't just explained that to them in her beautiful voice but had also remembered to perform for the audience, proving how calm she really was.

Elletear embodied the qualities of a true princess. She had practically no weak spots. She was perfect.

"Sh-she's stiff competition." Sisbell shuddered. "I might not be able to win this paired with someone like you, Alice!"

"And who was the one who flubbed the first question right away?!"

It was still too early to give up, though. Even though they'd already been shown up, they couldn't wave the white flag here without admitting they were failures as princesses.

"Defense Prime Minister!"

"Right now, I'm just a host."

"Th-then, Mr. Host! Please tell us what the next topic is!"

"Oh, looks like Princess Aliceliese is already hoping to challenge her sister back! That's great. What a wonderful contest between lovely princesses!"

"That's enough!"

"The next part of the competition is a battle of the arts."

There it is. I knew it would come!

"I've been waiting for this!" Alice balled her fists.

She had imagined this would happen.

This whole thing had started because of a fight between her and Sisbell about art, so she had been certain this would show up.

"It's too bad I won't be able to face off against you this time, Sisbell."

"Oh? Based on your confidence, Alice, I take it that you've trained a lot."

"Of course."

Since the initial argument over their paintings, Alice had sketched at least once daily. She knew she had improved for sure. Her one misgiving was that Elletear was also good at visual art…

"I'm confident. I put my blood, sweat, and tears into training—"

"All right, everyone put your aprons on."

"Aprons?"

"The theme of this part of the competition is the arts. In this case, the culinary arts!"

"We're cooking?!"

"Yes, gastronomy is considered an art these days."

This was bad.

Alice looked at Sisbell and found that her sister was also blanching.

"By the way, how are your cooking skills, Alice?"

"I have none…"

Princesses never cooked. The palace already had a chef. The most Alice could do was peel an apple.

Then what about Elletear?

......She just gave out cookies.

......And they were homemade, too.

That was proof she knew how to cook. This would be a difficult bout.

"Now, we've brought all kinds of ingredients from the palace kitchen!"

The bounties of the sea and mountains were brought in on trays.

"The theme is a dish fit for a princess. You have an hour. Start!"

"That's too soon!"

"We don't even have time to think of a recipe!"

Sisbell and Alice quickly donned aprons, but they had no idea what to make.

As they were doing this...

"Right. I'll whip up *that*."

...Elletear insinuated she had something up her sleeve, then headed over to find her ingredients.

She picked up some eggs.

"Alice! We should do the duel with eggs, too."

"Great idea, Sisbell! You must know a ton about egg recipes. "

Her little sister was suspiciously quiet.

"Then you were just getting ahead of yourself?!"

Alice had picked up two eggs. She didn't even have enough ideas to debate over which recipe to choose from. She could boil an egg or make an omelet.

That was all Alice had learned from the chef.

"Oh. But I made pudding with Rin before. Hey, Sisbell, are you—"

"Yeeek!"

As she carried an egg in each hand, Sisbell screamed and tripped.

"Ahh! I broke the eggs, and my head feels sticky?!"

Alice was too bewildered to say anything.

"Don't just stare, Alice, help me! We've joined forces, so we need to work together. One plus one is two. That's the power of teamwork!"

"You're just bringing me down, so it's one minus one equals zero!"

They cleaned up the floor. While they were working on that, time rapidly ticked down.

They had forty minutes left.

Elletear hummed as she continued to work.

"Urgh…the eggs are so slippery and hard. I can't seem to cut one."

Sisbell was attempting to cut into the eggshells.

"What are you doing?" Alice asked.

"I'm trying to get the shells off these eggs, of course. That's what the knife is for."

"You don't need one of those. See, you crack it against something flat, like a table… Hi-yah!"

Sisbell's eyes went wide.

"What an unprecedented method of shelling an egg!"

"Sisbell, you've never cooked before, have you?"

"Hah! Of all the things you could have said."

She brushed aside her shiny strawberry blond hair.

"Despite how I may look, I'm actually very discerning when it comes to flavors."

"That just means you know how to eat! Wait, we're running out of time!"

They had only raw eggs in front of them.

In other words, they hadn't made any progress.

"Sisbell, I'm going to crack the eggs and mix them, so you heat them up in the microwave!"

"I'm not sure how to use it!"

"You really are a useless princess, you know that?!"

Alice couldn't cook, either, but she'd never met anyone who was so inept that they couldn't use a microwave.

Sisbell must have been the most sheltered girl in the world.

"Okay, ten minutes left."

"Oh no… Oh nooo!"

Time passed relentlessly.

Alice worked the hardest she could.

"And that's time!" the minister's voice boomed. "Let's see the results. Princess Elletear made a golden egg mille-feuille cake. This'll be a hit with all the women in the audience! As for Princesses Alice and Sisbell…"

The entire place went silent.

On Alice and Sisbell's table was an egg that hadn't even been shelled…

"It's a boiled egg."

They'd worked very hard to get to that point.

Because of Sisbell, they'd had to quickly change recipes. This was the only thing Alice had known how to make in the time they'd had left.

"……Whew." Sisbell let out a light sigh.

"I thought you would be a bit more useful, Alice."

"I should be saying that to you!"

They'd fought bravely, but the results of the battle were out.

So far, their princess battle had tested their proficiency in culture (through a quiz) and the arts (gastronomy). Elletear had anticipated both and won.

"Now, this is our last large fight."

"What?"

The audience was getting excited.

When the host said that, Alice and Sisbell exchanged glances.

Hadn't they lost?

"The further we go into the competition, the more points each part is worth. The culture section was worth one point, and the art section was two. The final one will be…"

"Three, right?"

"…ten points!"

"Then why did we do any of that stuff earlier?!"

But this meant they were still in the running. Or rather, it would be possible for them to reverse the course of events spectacularly.

"Alice, do you think this is a chance to turn things around?"

"I do, Sisbell. The topic of the last battle will decide our fate. Well, host, what is the final one?!"

"That would be grace!"

A clothes locker was brought in. In it were opulent dresses from famous Sovereignty brands.

"This competition is about who can dress themselves the most beautifully. You need fashion and a sense of taste. In other words, a graceful outer appearance! Whoever does best overall will win!"

"Appearance?"

"Fashion?"

"Huh? What's wrong, Princesses Alice and Sisbell?"

They both seemed discouraged.

"*Haaah…*" Alice let out a heavy sigh and nodded at her sister.

"Let's go home, Sisbell."

"Yes, you're right…"

"It's tough when you've lost your will to fight. Are you okay—?"

Just then, they heard an easygoing voice call out from the changing room.

"Okay, I've changed. What do you all think?"

As her thick emerald hair fluttered behind her, Elletear came out in her adornments.

It only took one look at her to see what had happened.

"Oh, I see…"

Everyone understood now.

This was impossible.

"Hee-hee. I've never worn this dress before, so it's a little tight around the chest but cute nonetheless."

She grinned softly. Elletear had come out wearing a crimson dress with a daring slit that showed off her thighs. Her eyes were filled with affection and dignity, and her wavy emerald hair was so very attractive.

She was as beautiful as a siren, and she emanated a stately, mature air.

The audience went quiet.

They had all been so charmed by her appearance that they'd been left speechless.

"See, I knew it…"

"I thought this would happen…"

Alice and Sisbell had never stood a chance.

Not against their sister's "allure." Of course, the two sisters were also among the most beautiful girls in the Sovereignty, but Elletear's beauty was almost otherworldly.

"When Elletear really tries to dress up, she could steal the hearts of the entire audience here."

"We never had a chance in this category."

They snuck out of the hall. No one noticed that they had left.

"Thank you so much, everyone. As an encore, shall I change into the next outfit?"

Elletear started a solo fashion show.

"Ahh. If only you were just a little more dependable, Alice..."

"I should be saying that to you!"

The sisters' fight quietly echoed throughout the hallway.

3

The night.

"I can't accept this!" Alice said immediately after starting a postmortem meeting with her attendant, Rin. "It wasn't fair they made that the theme for the last part. No one can win against Elletear's allure!"

"If I may, I believe you are one of the most beautiful women in the Sovereignty, Lady Alice."

In other words, the issue had been the competition. Alice had been prepared for an obstacle, but Elletear had created a blockade that was too high for her to cross.

"You'll need another three years before you're as mature as her, Lady Alice."

"Uhh... I tried to compete against her too soon. But that's just who Elletear is."

"You put up a brave fight."

"...Really?"

"Yes. You had a 0.02 percent chance of winning, after all."

"Rin, you dummy!"

Alice put her head on the table. She could make no excuses for losing the culture and the arts sections of the competition. Elletear had worked for her successes.

"...Ahh. If only the last section had been a duel between young ladies. One based on the rules of the battlefield, where we could use our astral powers."

"Then you would be the overwhelming victor, Lady Alice. That has nothing to do with a princess's grace, though."

"You could have stopped before that last bit, you know!"

Alice considered calling it a night, but then Rin sat down in front of her.

"Oh. I do have one piece of good news, Lady Alice."

"What's that?"

"The audience loved this event."

"That's only because of Elletear, though. "

"No, they loved all three of you."

"Huh?"

"They liked how close you seemed."

The three princesses.

Normally they were busy and apart.

And the oldest was usually traveling around, so she was rarely at the palace.

......*Come to think of it.*

......*I haven't talked to them that much in a while.*

In that light, the event hadn't been too bad.

"That's exactly it!"

Suddenly, Alice rose from her desk.

"Giving the people something to feel happy about is one of a princess's duties! I would gladly do whatever I can to achieve that!"

"Then I have more good news for you, Lady Alice."

She had been waiting for this. Rin's eyes glittered.

"Because it was so well received, the event will take place on a regular basis. The second one is happening next month."

"That was decided without consulting me?!"

"Her Majesty wanted it."

"Mother did?!"

"Yes. But at this rate, you won't have any chance of winning, Lady Alice, so she ordered you to study harder for next time to put up a better fight."

"Nooo, I don't wanna study!"

She'd had enough.

Alice cried out as Rin brought a stack of textbooks to her.

File XX

The Strongest Combatants Serving the Lord

Our Last CRUSADE OR THE RISE OF A New World

Secret File

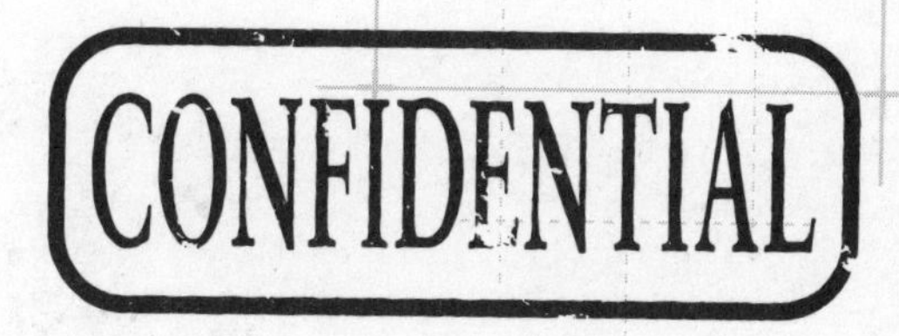

1

The Imperial capital.

The Mechanical Utopia, the center of the Empire, the home of several Imperial bases used in the Imperial forces' fight against the Nebulis Sovereignty.

Wintertime had come to the capital.

"It's already the end of the year..."

Imperial forces, Third Base.

Commander Mismis rested her head on the conference room table as she relaxed.

"It's cold outside because of the winds blowing in from the north, and the department stores are bustling from the year-end sales. What classic winter scenes. Now we just wait for the end of the year."

"Mismis, I think you're getting a little ahead of yourself," said someone by the window.

Risya gave them a strained smile as she took her eyes off the soldiers' winter training exercise.

"You have two days left until winter holidays start," she said.

"Yeah, just two more days!"

They were both more or less saying the same words with the exact opposite sentiments. While Risya was still fulfilling her duties as part of the top brass, Mismis was already preoccupied with making holiday plans.

"Right… I got my winter bonus in already. Now all I need to do is enjoy my break to its fullest."

"You're acting like you're already on vacation." Risya let out an exasperated sigh. "I still have tons of work to do, so I can't get in the holiday mood yet. By the way, what are your end-of-year plans like, Mismis?"

"They're perfect this year!"

She seemed very happy to have been asked. Mismis beamed and jumped out of her seat. "First, I'm going to watch all the TV shows I recorded this year! I'll sit under my heated table and watch them while eating end-of-year BBQ—"

"You can't!"

"What?"

"Do you think an Imperial soldier is allowed to slack off like that?!" Risya suddenly barked. She charged right up to Mismis, who gaped at her friend. "A winter break is meant for preparing for the coming year. You should be using the time to better yourself!"

"Uh, Risya, even the commanding officers said to use the break to mentally relax…"

"Those were all lies."

"What?!"

"How you spend this winter break will determine how the rest of the year goes—and that's no overstatement. This isn't the time for mental relaxation!" Risya grabbed Mismis's shoulders. "Anyone can get themselves to work for the sake of others at any time of the year. For example…the people who deliver the New Year's letters. They keep working through the holidays without going on break!"

"Th-this seems like a different topic entirely?"

"They're a huge deal. You're going to send New Year's letters, too, right, Mismis?"

"Yeah…just a few."

Now, New Year's letters were simply postcards sent for the new year. They were meant to reach their recipients on the first day of January. However, they'd increased in popularity lately, which had started causing delivery issues.

"The delivery workers are giving up their breaks to make sure everyone gets their mail. Isn't that right?"

"……Y-yeah. The delivery workers are amazing. They drive around the entire capital on New Year's Day in their cars and on their motorcycles without sleeping or resting…"

"Are you grateful for their service?"

"Of course!"

"Do you respect them?"

"Uh, sure…but it's not respect so much as that I'm just impressed…"

"Then it's decided." Risya smiled. "Mismis, how about you do some deliveries, then?"

"…What?"

"Well, you're grateful for their service, aren't you? And you respect them—the letter delivery workers, that is."

"What? Wait, Risya, what's going on with you?! What's that look in your eyes…?" Mismis had noticed too late. Even though

Risya was grinning at her as she kept a vise grip over Mismis's shoulders, the smile didn't reach her eyes.

"R-Risya?!"

"Hee-hee. I have my reasons for this."

A few hours earlier.

The Lord's offices.

The windowless building was known as the Lord's residence. Currently, the most prominent leaders of the Imperial forces were gathered in a room.

First were the top brass from headquarters. Then there were the generals from Divisions I to VI. The most highly regarded of all were the Saint Disciples, who served the Lord directly.

As everyone gathered in the space, the Lord watched the scene from afar through a camera.

They were coming up with plans for next year's military operations.

"All right."

Over fifty people were gathered around the circular table.

One of the people in charge of the headquarters's business affairs stood up while holding a thick stack of documents.

"That concludes the last meeting of the year. See you all next year."

They'd *just* finished.

The entire group of fifty headed out to leave. One member of the crowd, Risya, slowly stretched.

"Ahh…I'm so tired. Seven-hour meetings with no break really are suffocating affairs."

But this was also her final one of the year. The other top brass leaving the hall also seemed relieved, like a weight had been lifted off them upon finishing their last big job.

Then again...

Risya still had lots of things she needed to take care of.

She was the fifth seat of the Saint Disciples and also a special headquarters employee. She had her work cut out for her.

"Looks like it's another day of overtime... I still need to go over those strategy documents."

It seemed she would be welcoming the new year while working—yet again. She was on a strict schedule—a death march, really. If only she had a secretary to keep her organized through her brutal itinerary.

"Oh, I know! Hey, Shuri!"

"What is it, Ms. Risya?"

A bespectacled office worker turned around when Risya called her name. She was the budget officer of headquarters, Shurilia. Though she was new and had been assigned to headquarters only recently, she was busier than anyone else at that moment because it was the time of year for fiscal budgeting.

"You look so relieved, Shuri," Risya said to her.

"That's because I am..." The woman, who was young enough to look like a college student, let out a sigh. "For the past month, I've been putting together the documents we need to create the budget. I've spent night after night on the base... I haven't even had time to take a proper bath, and I eventually stopped doing makeup. My suit was full of wrinkles, too, and I barely felt like a woman while I was living like that. But it's all over with today."

"Uh-huh, sure. Sounds like you can rest easy and welcome the new year."

"Yes!"

"So I've got a favor I need to ask you."

"Which would be…?"

"Could you put in a teeny, little correction for me in my budget?"

Crack. As soon as Risya said that, Shurilia froze over.

"See, I've just drowning in work. It'd help a ton if I had a secretary to help me manage my schedule. Even more so if they could make me tea and meals."

Shurilia was completely silent.

"I'm sure someone with as much say as you could fiddle with the budget numbers a little to fit a secretary in for me. Right… huh, Shuri?"

"Oh? Wh-what was I doing?!" Shurilia seemed to come back to her senses. "I-I'm sorry. I've slept so little that I must have blacked out for a moment. It sounded like you were asking for the budget for a secretary last-minute, but I'm sure I was just mishearing things. A smart person like yourself would never request something so ridiculous…"

"No, I did."

"Please tell me you're joking!" The documents in her hands fluttered to the ground. "I can't! It's impossible! Completely impossible! We just got the budget approved, too!"

"But I just remembered it now. You can do it, can't you?"

"I can't put more strain on myself! Even for a special employee of the headquarters! So I'll be going now. I still have a mountain of work to do today."

She quickly gathered all the papers on the floor and turned to leave. But as she tried to get away from Risya…

"Yo, Shu, I've got a little request for you."

"Ms. Mei?" Shurilia stopped in her tracks as another officer approached her from the side.

This person was another Saint Disciple, just like Risya. She was the third seat of the Saint Disciples, the incessant storm Mei. She'd come from Special Division V, which the Empire dispatched to underdeveloped lands.

As such, she had honed her skills in merciless environments and roughed it out for her training. Her long hair was a tangled mess, and her skin was sunbaked, giving her the appearance of a wild lion.

"Um, Ms. Mei, this might be rude of me, but..."

"Hm? What is it?"

"You're rarely the last one around at these meetings."

It wasn't odd for Shurilia to be suspicious. Mei's hatred of meetings was infamous. She couldn't stand sitting still and would practically dash out of the room as soon as one was done. So why was she lingering in the hall?

What for?

"That's because I have something to ask you, Shu."

"Me specifically?"

"Yeah. So, Shu, *I actually have a favor to ask you.*"

"Huh?!" The budget manager flinched and shivered. And little wonder. Risya had just said almost the exact same thing. "Y-you're not going to ask..."

"Could you bump up Division V's funds a bit? And if you could keep it a secret from the other departments, that'd be great."

"You too?!"

"Aw, I wanna buy a huge tank for next year. One that's just for me."

"You want it all to yourself?!"

"C'mon, it'll only cost a little."

"It most certainly won't be just a 'little'! First there was Risya and now this. Why didn't you ask during the meeting?!"

"I was asleep."

"You were what?!" The budget officer staggered. "M-my precious meeting...that I spent a month preparing for..."

"Oh, c'mon, Shu. If you look at page eighteen, Division VI is getting twice the budget per head of Division V."

"Oh, so you did go through those."

"So why do they have twice as much? If you can give a wad of cash to those sneaky guys skulking in the shadows where nobody can even see their work, why can't you give us a little—"

Someone interrupted Mei before she could finish.

"What a funny joke."

A man was standing directly behind her. He wore a strange, dull-colored, suit-like outfit that covered him from head to toe.

"So, Mei, what was it that you were saying about Division VI?"

"Eep!" Shurilia turned around in shock when she realized someone had approached her from behind without a sound. "M-Mr. Nameless!"

"———"

He was Saint Disciple of the eighth seat, Nameless. Like Mei and Risya, he was the Lord's guard. He came from Special Division VI, which operated from the shadows, conducting covert missions that their coworkers, much less the general populace, wouldn't have any way of knowing about. In other words, they were the assassin unit.

Nameless was also one of the top soldiers from the division.

"So, Mei, which unit exactly is 'sneaky' and 'skulking' in the shadows?"

"Ha-ha. Don't get all knotted up about it, Names. Unless this is your way of telling me I hit the mark?"

The tall man looked down on Mei, towering over her. She snickered as though she was enjoying that.

"You're always sneaking around the base and battlefields; meanwhile Division V is roughing it out there. That's what I'm talking about."

"Oh?"

"Besides, we aren't just going up against witches in our division. Have you ever sunk into a bottomless swamp in the savage jungle? Or gotten surrounded by a gang of basilisks while lost in the desert? Only the top 7 percent of those who take the forces test to get in are allowed into Division V. We're the true elite forces."

"Ah yes, Division V, which only requires a physical test to get in." Nameless pulled no punches. *"In mission performance, Division VI seeks soldiers with a variety of abilities: physical prowess, learning ability, and adaptability. But you just want soldiers who are physically strong? That's all Division V specializes in? You might as well have gorillas fulfill your missions."*

"How dare you!"

"Division VI is an independent unit that no other department can meddle with. We are tasked with protecting a large number of state secrets and making sure nothing leaks. We can't allow for even a single mistake in our missions. And you think your division could compare to us… Hah!"

Nameless laughed. He wasn't just adding fuel to the fire at this point—this was throwing dynamite into an oil field.

"How can you even say you're putting your lives at risk when all you do is wander around places where no one lives?"

"Well, now you've done it, Names." Mei daringly stared at him. "In that case—"

"P-please wait!" Shurilia quickly broke into their dispute. She pushed up the bridge of her glasses. "Really, now… It won't do to fight in a place like this. We can't have discord between Divisions V and VI. HQ wouldn't want that. Please bury the hatchet."

"So you'll increase my division's budget?"

"Only under certain conditions." A glint flashed in the timid woman's eyes as her attitude reversed. "We've received budget increase requests from all three of you. I can't simply give you extra funds, but I could pay you for a part-time job."

"A part-time job?"

"Making the New Year's letter deliveries this year. I was going to ask another department to help, but I can request that you do it instead."

She pulled three pieces of paper from her thick stack of documents.

Then she handed the sheets of paper to the three of them.

"Take a look at this graph that tracks the number of letters sent each year. We've seen a sevenfold increase in the last four years. This is partially a result of giveaway cards that include the opportunity to win luxurious prizes, like a brand-new car or a mansion and vacation home. There are so many cards being sent out these days that over three hundred million are delivered in the capital alone."

"Hey, Shu," Mei said as she looked up from the document. She also sighed. "You're not telling us to deliver these cards ourselves, are you?"

"That is exactly right," she said.

"Then it's just a regular old part-time job! Why would you ask us to do that...?"

"What if I said that the team that delivers the most cards will get a special bonus?"

"Huh!" Mei's eyes twitched. "...I see. So that's how we'd get our budget increase."

"Please be careful with your phrasing. HQ can't give out budget increases, but we do have some leeway when it comes to compensating part-time work."

"I'm in, Shuri!" Risya thumped Shurilia on the back and nodded enthusiastically. "So if I win, I'll get a secretary. That'll be easy. Most of Division V isn't even in the capital, and there aren't many members of Division VI anyway. All I've got to do is use my personal connections to overwhelm the competition with numbers."

"Geez, Risya, don't act like you've already won." Mei grinned, her canines glinting. "You forget it's the end of the year. Some of my people are back in the capital right now. All I've gotta do is get them mobilized, and this win is in the bag for me."

"Hee-hee. Do you really think that, Ms. Mei?"

Risya and Mei glared at each other. Meanwhile, the man representing Division VI didn't bother to hide his sigh.

"How foolish..."

He left the paper on a desk and turned his back to them.

"I have no desire to wag my tail for headquarters. Mei, Risya, you do what you want—"

"Oh, Names?"

"Scared of losing, are you?"

"Heh-heh."

The two Saint Disciples whispered loudly so he could hear.

"Say, Risya, that doesn't sound like something a real man would do."

"You're completely right. What Saint Disciple would run from a fight? Right, Ms. Mei?"

"———"

The Saint Disciple of the eighth seat remained silent. Eventually, he let out a second sigh.

"Fine. If you insist on blatantly provoking me, then I'll take you up on your challenge."

Thus, the battle between headquarters, Division V, and Division VI started.

"So there you have it. It happened a few hours ago." Risya nodded to herself. "Basically, it's a chance for me to get the budget I need for a secretary. Now let's talk strategy. Mismis, you'll be on First Street in the capital."

"I haven't said I'd accep—ngh?!"

"Listen, Mismis!" Risya clapped her hand over Mismis's mouth. "This may seem like a fight over the budget at first glance. But it's not. This is bigger than that. It's a dispute between the factions in the Imperial forces. A standoff between Division V, VI, and headquarters. And the results will be merciless. Our pride is on the line!"

"That's way too dramatic!"

"It really isn't. We're deciding which faction is the most competent. The one that wins will have a lot to be proud of. I need to win this before the year ends!"

"Can't you just have a normal New Year's?!"

As Risya became more impassioned, Commander Mismis deflated.

As for the audience watching the whole thing…

"I agree with Commander Mismis," Iska said.

"Me too," Nene added.

"Looks like we've got no choice anyway…," Jhin also said. The three of them glanced at one another.

It was right before the end of the year, and every unit in the

Imperial forces was prepping for the coming year. They'd wondered what why Risya was dropping by for a visit when she should have been busy, too.

"Do you think she's going to drag us into it, too…?"

"You've got that right, Isk! When you're in the 907, you're in it together!" Risya spread her arms out. "When a commander's in a predicament, she needs to be supported by her troops! That's the beauty of the forces! We all support one another!"

"But you're the reason why I'm in a predicament, Risya!"

"Hmm. So I think I've got about two hundred people now."

Apparently, Iska and the others were already helping out in Risya's mind. The fact that she'd drafted two hundred soldiers into her service during what should have been a break was also a surprise.

"Ms. Risya, even if you want a secretary really badly, I don't think you can just order the troops around like this willy-nilly…"

"Hee-hee. It just goes to show how popular I am, Isk." Risya didn't hesitate at all to admit it. "I'm sure Nameless and Ms. Mei are going about delivering postcards the wrong way. The right way to do this is to overwhelm with sheer numbers by sending in a huge wave of people. The person who gathers the most people—"

"I don't think it will go as smoothly as you planned."

"Waaah?!" Mismis fell off her chair.

Suddenly, an assassin in a suit appeared directly behind her. She was sure no one had been there a second ago.

"Hm. I wondered who you all were. So it's your *unit."*

He turned off his optical camouflage. Nameless stared at Iska and the others.

They had met before.

Iska's unit was from Special Division III. On the other hand, Nameless had worked his way up from Division VI into becoming a Saint Disciple. Though they were in different divisions, they had once worked together when trying to strategize to steal a vortex.

"So you've decided to become Risya's dogs. Well, it's the same as if she'd recruited anyone else."

"Hey, Risya, I'm here to see what the enemy's up to." The door opened, and a feral-looking female soldier took long strides into the room. As soon as Risya saw the woman, she gave her a strained smile.

"Oh, now even you're here, Ms. Mei?"

"Looks like you're still plugging away at scouting, Risya. I heard you collected over a hundred…hm?"

Mei turned to look at Mismis, Jhin, and Nene until her eyes finally landed on Iska. She was the third seat of the Saint Disciples, and Iska had once been a Saint Disciple, too. They'd never spoken before, but they knew of each other.

"Who're you again? Oh, right, you're Aska."

"It's Iska."

"So they released you, huh? Or did Risya get you out? Hey, Risya, did you really go that far just for some letter deliveries?"

"I didn't have anything to do with getting him acquitted, and that happened a long time ago."

"Oh? Well, who cares?" Mei really seemed to have come by just to see what was up. She nodded with satisfaction and turned right around. "Unfortunately for you, Risya, no matter how many people you recruit, Division V is still going to win."

"One hundred? Two hundred? In the end, you just have a random assortment of people, and no teamwork to speak of."

Nameless made his exit after Mei. Iska and the others watched them both leave.

"No way!" Risya held up her fist and yelled back, "I'm going to be the one to win! Mismis promised me I would!"

"Don't bring me into this!"

2

End of year, 11:30 p.m.

Unit 907 was gathered at conference room in a base.

"Ahh…" Commander Mismis let out a weak sigh from where she was facedown on the table. "There are thirty minutes until the new year Normally, I'd be watching New Year's programs while eating BBQ in front of the TV right about now…"

"Don't you watch TV and eat BBQ whenever?"

"You don't get it, Jhin!" Commander Mismis caught Jhin's comment and stood up. "Watching TV and eating BBQ at the end of the year makes me super-duper happy!"

"So you're *not* happy with the BBQ you always eat on a regular basis?"

"No, I am!"

"Then it's the same."

"It's not!"

As he watched their exchange from the side, Iska headed over to the door when the interphone rang. "Commander, looks like they're here."

He opened the door to find shipping boxes piled in the hallway. The boxes were large enough to block almost all access—and there were three of them.

"Huh? Are these all New Year's letters?!" Naturally, Nene was taken aback when she looked up at the boxes, too.

There were three hundred million postcards being delivered

just in the capital alone. At first Iska hadn't fully believed it, but now that he was staring at the containers in front of him, it all started feeling real.

"So we need to deliver all of these before five in the morning, Iska?"

"Looks like there's a reason why they want us to do delivery."

This must have been why the Imperial forces had been recruited to help.

As Iska and the others realized they would need to really dedicate themselves to the task if they were going to be successful, Risya cheerfully made her way over to them. "Yoo-hoo, Mismis. Wow, so you've all been waiting here. That's great."

Right behind her was an office worker lugging in another box.

"Here, there are seven more, too."

"This is impossible!"

As Mismis yelled, even more boxes were being piled in the hallway up to the ceiling. It looked like there were about ten in total. They had to wonder how many tens of thousands of letters were stuffed in those giant containers.

"That's a lot..."

"No wonder they want us to help deliver them..."

"This is impossible. We can't finish delivering these by daybreak."

Nene and Iska broke into a cold sweat. Behind them, Jhin was already musing about the future. "Hey, Ms. Saint Disciple, the four of us can't deliver all of these."

"It's okay if you can't manage them all."

"What?"

"Jhinjhin, did you forget this is a competition? The whole point is to deliver as many cards as we can to beat the other two teams."

Risya pulled out a small LCD monitor from her pocket.

On it was some text that read: MEI'S TEAM: 0, RISYA'S TEAM: 0, NAMELESS'S TEAM: 0.

"We're using this device to measure how many we deliver in real time. It's 11:58. In two minutes, it'll all kick off."

They would begin at midnight on the dot and head out of the base just as the new year started. Then they would just be competing for better numbers. Risya's, Mei's, and Nameless's teams would see how many letters they could deliver by five in the morning.

"Okay, 907, I've gotten some bags ready for you, so stuff as many letters as you can into these!"

They did exactly as Risya told them. Once they had the backpacks on, they were ready to go.

"Thirty seconds left…twenty…nineteen…eighteen…" Risya started her countdown. Mei's and Nameless's people were probably also on standby around the capital.

"Five, four, three, two, one…start! Okay, off you go, Mismis!"

"Okay, okay, let's get going, everyone!" Commander Mismis ran out, practically desperate to get this over with.

The gates to the base opened, and she gallantly ran out…

…only to be met with a raging snowstorm standing in her way.

The world outside was pitch-black from the storm.

"What is this…?" Mismis said to herself. As she stopped to gape, snow collected on her shoulders and head.

"Looks like a blizzard."

"Oh, I think I saw something about this on the weather report—there was a chance of snow."

"That's why I said this would be impossible."

No one could have predicted a New Year's snowstorm. The Imperial capital rarely got snow to begin with. But enough of it had come down to reach Mismis's knees, and the entire base was already covered in white.

"Ha..." Commander Mismis let out a strained laugh. "Maybe we should give up."

"Already?! Commander, it's too early just to call it quits!"

"This is impossible, Iska! Impossible, I tell you!" Commander Mismis vehemently shook her head from side to side. "I've never seen a snowstorm like this before. This is a huge disaster! Look, I've got snow reaching up to my butt!"

"Oh no... This was completely unexpected." Risya also looked displeased at the sight. She seemed to be getting news from a direct report through the comm at her ear. "Looks like none of the delivery trucks can move because of this snow. The trains and taxis are stopped, too. The two hundred deliverers can't get out of the base..."

It was ten minutes past midnight now. Risya's team had made zero deliveries so far. Mei and Nameless's teams likely hadn't, either. At least, everyone there believed that.

"Huh?! What?"

The small monitor Risya was looking at had shown some movement. The other divisions' numbers had started rising abruptly. They were already making multiple hundreds of deliveries.

"What's going on? Hey, you guys doing counts, could you put up footage? Send me footage of the other divisions' deliveries."

Risya's monitor switched to another image.

That was when they witnessed a shocking scene from the surveillance cameras set up around the capital.

The Imperial capital, Sector Two, Fourth Street.

The intersection was clogged with cars that were at a standstill owing to the heavy snow. There were families trying to get to their parents' homes to celebrate the new year, and couples attempting to get out of the capital to see the first sunrise of the year.

"Ugh! The traffic's horrible because of the snow!"

"The car in the front skidded out and caused an accident. There's a tow truck coming."

"I heard the tow truck is being blocked by the snow, too..."

The intersections were all like scenes from hell.

None of the cars were budging in this weather. Since the passengers were also stuck, they hadn't been able to use the restroom or eat, either.

"Yeah, our New Year's is completely ruined... Damn it."

Everyone muttered complaints as they huddled in their vehicles, feeling exhaustion creeping in.

But just then, something slipped right by the cars.

Fwoosh, fwoosh. Black shadows zipped between the stopped vehicles.

Whatever those things were, there weren't just one or two of them.

"Hm? Huh? Was that just my eyes tricking me...?" One of the fathers rubbed his eyes as he sat in the driver's seat.

No vehicles could have gotten anywhere in this blizzard. That was what he was telling himself, at least.

Thump.

"Whoaaa?!"

His family screamed, which was a natural reaction, really—someone had just jumped onto the hood of his car.

To be more precise, several random men wearing Imperial-issue coats and snow goggles were standing on the hood.

"Don't move," one said.

"D-don't move?! Wait, we're just normal people—"

"This is a white, eighth-gen compact car of Imperial make with a capital plate number of 0918. Mei, I've got the target!"

"Good job, my little commanderino."

Another female soldier landed on the hood of the car with a thump. No one would have guessed she was the Saint Disciple Mei. On top of that, everyone on her team was wearing goggles, so no one could tell who they were. The family assumed that her squad was about to rough them up in a vehicle holdup.

"C-call the police! No, the Imperial forces!"

"You've already got the Imperial forces right here," one of the soldiers said.

"Excuse me?"

"You're Hoit Maclauren, and you live at 9 Fourth Street in apartment fourteen. That means the woman in the passenger seat is Anna Maclauren. Is that right?"

"Wh-who are you all?! You're part of the forces?!" the man demanded.

"We have something nice for you." Mei smiled, showing a peek of her canines. She pulled something out of her pocket. "Here you go. These are your New Year's letters."

"......Come again?"

"You and your wife have forty-three in total. And you're headed to her parents' house, right?"

"H-how did you know?!"

"I'll hand the cards meant for your wife's parents to you, too. There are fifty-four of them. All right, that's nearly a hundred all at once. Let's get to the next one."

"Uh, um?!"

Ignoring the man, Mei and her team turned around and slid right through the snow-covered intersection. They were on skis and snowboards.

"Commanderino, what's the next target?" Mei asked.

"A big red car stopped just around the corner!"

"Ha-ha, this is way too easy."

Mei slid through the intersection on a snowboard.

Yes. Cars, motorcycles, and bikes were as good as immobile in knee-high snow. But skis and snowboards were perfect for blizzards. They could slide between the stalled vehicles without issue.

"Hee-hee. Risya and Names will have no idea what hit them. Division V operates in remote regions. We've got training to deal with heavy snow, too."

Division V had traveled through undeveloped snowy landscapes on dogsleds and skis. A little blizzard was child's play for them.

"Plus, the snow's blocking all the intersections. That means that some of the recipients are going to be in their cars. That's a few hundred vehicles. And it's efficient."

"Ms. Mei!" The commander skiing behind her called out. "We've secured this intersection (finished the deliveries) and have pretty much handed out everything we can!"

"Good job, my little commanderino. But we can't let our guards down until we dominate this mission and are the last ones standing. Let's head to the next location."

Mei took her subordinates with her to the next spot. Their target was a large condo building. That would allow them to get a lot more deliveries done at once.

The blizzard probably wouldn't die down for a while longer,

which meant Risya's and Nameless's teams were probably still stuck at the base.

"Hee-hee. I almost feel bad it's this easy."

With a sympathetic smile on her face, Mei checked the delivery statistics. Risya's team was still at 0. However…

"What? Names has already done 4,697 deliveries?!"

She doubted her eyes.

Mei's team was currently at 5,191, so they were neck and neck. The number for Nameless's team had also been ticking up the entire time she'd been looking at it. He was managing that in this blizzard?

He wouldn't be able to use cars or motorcycles, and the trains were stopped. Helicopters couldn't fly in this weather, either, of course. How was he getting these numbers, then?

"You put up a tough fight, Names. Wonder what trick you've got up your sleeve."

Mei smiled boldly as she looked down at the delivery stats.

Around the same time.

A restaurant in the capital.

Even with the snow falling, restaurants and cafés were still bustling with couples celebrating the new year.

"Wow, this was a great New Year's dinner."

"I still want a little more to drink."

"We can go to one of my regular bars, then. There's this place I know really well."

"But it's been snowing."

"We can walk. It's right there." *C'mon.* The young man gave his date a gentlemanly smile and tugged on her hand. "Our love can overcome anything. Not even snow can block our path."

"That's so beautiful!"

The couple started walking together, hand in hand. Or at least, they tried to.

At that moment, the snow right at their feet started to shift.

"Hm?"

Then there was an explosion.

A manhole flew up, and the snow and the boyfriend were sent shooting into the air along with it.

"Gaaah?!"

"Kailos? Are you okay, Kailos?! What happened to that manhole cover?!"

The woman's boyfriend had been knocked out after getting hit in the head with the manhole cover. She tried to run over to him. "I've got you."

But then suddenly she started to scream, "Ahhhhh?!"

Someone had grabbed her by the ankle as she was running to her boyfriend, and they were coming up from inside the manhole.

"St-stop! What are you?!" she cried out.

"I am forbidden to answer that question."

An armed soldier crawled out of the hole. Other men wearing goggles and masks also appeared from the underground sewer system. Their voices sounded artificial, altered by electrical equipment.

They went beyond suspicious—these men meant certain trouble.

"You're Marian Shimilla of Second Street, Seventh Ward, at residence twenty-three, I presume?"

"N-no! That's not me!"

"You cannot trick us."

The men marched across the snow.

"We have business with you."

"N-no, stay away from me. Someone, anyone, please help!"

"We are here to deliver your New Year's letters."

"D-don't come any closer!"

"Did you hear me? We are here to deliver your New Year's letters. You have seventeen of them."

"...........Excuse me?"

"Take them quickly."

The soldier had pulled out a stack of cards held together with a rubber band. He had two sets.

"The man next to you seems to be Kailos Graham of Second Street, Seventh Ward, residence thirty-one."

"..."

"Is that right or not?"

"...Y-yes, that's right," the woman said.

"Then this is for him. Twenty-one cards. We have delivered thirty-eight in total."

Taken aback, the young woman couldn't find it in her to reply.

Then the strange armed group turned around.

"Let's go. We'll continue to use the underground route."

They disappeared into the manhole.

"What was that...?"

She and her boyfriend had no way of knowing this, but the capital had an underground network that was disguised as a sewer system. Since snow was coming down from above, Nameless's team had simply used the underground system. This was the route he had chosen to use for the deliveries.

"Where is Nameless?"

"He's made it to the second point. We will continue to attac—I mean warmly deliver the letters at the bar in this establishment."

That night, the Imperial capital that was bustling with New Year's celebrations also rang out with screams. Citizens all over encountered a scene straight from a horror movie as strange armed men crawled out of manholes to deliver mail.

And now…

Mei's team had continued with their ski-and-snowboard strategy to deliver 9,091 letters. Nameless's team had used their underground route to deliver 8,989 cards. They were basically head-to-head.

In contrast, the headquarters team had still made a total of 0 deliveries.

"Oh nooo!"

They were at the entrance to the base. Risya was yelling as she held her head in her hands.

Iska had never seen her this upset before.

"I can't believe the snow caused such a mess… No, wait, we've gotten a late start and they're ahead, but we can still fix this. Okay, off you go, Mismis!"

"Uh, Risya." Mismis pointed at the mound of snow. "The cars and trains are stalled in this blizzard."

"Just run then!" Risya said.

"Run?!" Mismis's voice cracked as Risya pointed to the snow-covered landscape.

"Risya, that's just not—"

"Listen, Mismis. These letters are ringing in the new year for the citizenry. We're delivering the arrival of a new age; in other words, we're giving them hope itself. We *have* to complete the deliveries."

"Okay, but what are you really after?"

"I want a bigger budget. I don't want to be bested by the other two teams."

"See, I knew it!"

"But hope is a big deal, too!"

"But your ulterior motives are so obvious!"

"No, Mismis, listen closely. The other units have already left!"

They were outside the base. While Mismis was hemming and hawing, Risya had sent the others off to run into the storm. They were practically swimming through the snow and doing the butterfly stroke to get anywhere.

"Wow..."

"We lost contact with two units just earlier, though."

"They must have gotten into an accident, then!"

Soldiers were going down right in front of their eyes. Even though they were brawny Imperial soldiers, they were no match for the cold and the blizzard.

"Let's go, Mismis! We need to carry the souls who sacrificed themselves with us!"

"That's not a burden I want to carry!"

"No arguing! Come on, Unit 907, get out there! Isk, Jhinjhin, you two head to the first location. Nens, you keep in contact with them from here. Mismis and I will work together!"

"Noooo!"

After donning a winter coat, Risya dragged Mismis into the blizzard. Unit 907 listened to their commander's deathly wails.

"Oh, good. Looks like I get to stick to the base," Nene said.

"...Oh, c'mon. Let's go, Iska. We should get this over with quick."

"Right..."

Jhin and Iska ran into the snow together.

But they weren't running so much as expending all their energy just getting through the white powder. They were barely going faster than a normal walk, and they were exerting themselves much more than normal.

"So we're doing this all night long. This is hard labor..."

"Don't talk; you're using energy."

They silently made their way through the snow. Iska and Jhin arrived at a very tall condo. According to Risya, this was the most important location. If they delivered letters to this building, which contained countless households, they would be able to get rid of thousands of cards.

They went up to the entrance of the building.

As soon as Iska and Jhin were inside, they took the letters out of their backpack. There were hundreds of mailboxes in front of them.

"Iska, I'll start with number 1001 on floor one. You start with the highest floor."

"Okay."

They started their deliveries, checking the names and apartment numbers as they delivered the letters one after another.

"Oh? Looks like you made it, Isk, Jhinjhin. Our delivery total is 798 now. That's a good pace." Risya's voice came over the long-distance comm.

But Iska didn't have time to answer her. He had to keep concentrating. There were tons of families that had similar names in the gigantic condo building.

"Iska, careful. Apparently, a lot of mistakes happen in condo deliveries," Jhin murmured. They were thinking the same thing. "According to when I checked beforehand, Michelle is in Apartment 908."

"Okay."

"Even when it comes to Michelles, there's also a Michelle Haif Christof in 906. The first woman I was talking about is Michelle Haif *Marianne*, so be careful."

"What? Wait, say that again..."

"Michelle Haif Christof is in 906, and Michelle Haif Marianne is in 908."

"I—I think I get it..."

"No, I got that wrong. The first Michelle is in 905, the second is in 909, and this one isn't Michelle, it's a *Muchelle*."

"That's way too confusing!"

The next instant, Iska heard someone.

"Who's there?!" he called out.

"Looks like the target is in this high-rise."

However, there was no one there.

But then the spot the voice had come from quivered, and a man wearing a full optical camouflage suit appeared.

"Nameless..."

"By taking control of this location, you should be able to make a large number of deliveries. That commitment to efficiency is pure Risya." Nameless raised his arms as though to mock them. *"You're late. Division VI has already secured (completed deliveries to) all the other condos except this one. Giving people letters here won't change anything."*

"What?!"

That seemed too fast.

To deliver to all those condos in such a short span of time, they would have needed tens of thousands of soldiers. Division VI was known for being small.

"How did you do that? Even if condos are efficient, trying to deliver the letters without making mistakes takes time."

"The misdeliveries don't concern me."

"What?" Iska hadn't expected that answer.

"A difference of a single digit in an apartment number is within an acceptable margin of error."

"What?!"

"You seem to not understand what the point of this mission is." Nameless laughed. *"Our orders are simply to deliver the New Year's letters. But they never stipulated the accuracy of the task. So all we need to do is keep delivering."*

"I think you're really pushing it by doing that!"

"Tell Risya that she's already lost."

As Nameless tried to leave, his comm went off.

"What?"

"We have an emergency."

"I'll decide if it's an emergency. Give it to me."

"We've received a warning from HQ. We finished making deliveries to all the nearby condos. But because we neglected to check the identities of the recipients, there were more misdeliveries than expected. The forces have received a deluge of complaints."

"..........."

"After a review, they've decided not to count the misdeliveries."

Before Nameless's eyes, Division VI's count dropped from 90,000 to 60,000. *"Tsk. That's fine. Continue with the—"*

"Ah-ha-ha! Sounds like you're not in a good mood!"

They heard something slide through the snow. Mei had slid right into the condo building on her snowboard.

"Seems like you flubbed that last job, Names. "

"It's not an issue."

"Don't put up a brave front. Looks like this is the end of the competition, though. Division V finished handling the residential areas. Thanks to your little misfire, we've gained the lead. If we can just keep it up until five—hm?"

Mei tilted her head. The comm she was holding flashed just like Nameless's had earlier.

"Geez, what now? I'm busy. Yeah, what is it, Commanderino?"

"We have an emergency."

"I'll decide if it's an emergency."

Wait...

Iska and Jhin looked at each other and felt a strange sense of déjà vu. Even Nameless had noticed something was up and stared at Mei.

"What is it, Commanderino?"

"As we were heading north on Second Street, our whole unit was arrested..."

"What?!"

"...by traffic guards at an intersection."

"Wait, wait, that's not the important part! Tell me *why* they arrested us. What was their justification?!"

"Speeding."

"......?" Mei blinked. "Say that again, Commanderino."

"It was for speeding. The skis and snowboards were fine, but apparently the issue was where we were riding them. Within the capital, we're only allowed to go sixty kilometers per hour on public streets..."

"Shoot!" Mei's eyes went wide.

Division V mainly operated in remote regions. In the snowy outback, there were no speed limits. But they were on public roads now. They had to follow the streetlights and the speed limits. Mei had forgotten that.

"H-hey, Commanderino...what does that mean...?"

"We were massacred." The commander sounded grim over the comm. **"Actually, I'm speaking from an interrogation room at a station right now."**

"Even you?!"

She hadn't expected to lose all her people. Yet the flames of competition still burned in Mei's eyes.

"No...this doesn't change things! You still lost delivery numbers, Names. Even though I lost my people, I still have my numbers!"

Nameless's delivery numbers had grown from 60,000 to 70,000, but Mei's team had 90,000.

"And it's still only four fifteen a.m. You can't make up our lead in less than an hour."

She was both provoking him and declaring that victory was as good as hers.

Risya's voice came over Iska's comm.

"Ha-ha, you're naive, Ms. Mei."

"What?!"

"You neglected to check my team's delivery numbers."

"Huh?!" Mei checked her monitor and ground her teeth. Risya's numbers had grown to 80,000. She was catching up to Mei.

Iska and Jhin were flabbergasted. They knew that their numbers were being added in, but that didn't account for the large sum.

"Ms. Risya? How did you do this?!"

"Ha-ha. I suppose I could share my secret with you. I just borrowed some new drones from the weapons development department. They can fly in rough weather."

"And then what?"

"I had them airdrop the letters to people's doorsteps."

"That sounds like cheating!"

"Nens is actually the one handling them. I left her at the base because I thought this might happen."

"You could have just used the drones to begin with!"

"I only just went out to borrow them."

Risya didn't even blink at Iska's comment.

They could hear the sounds of footsteps in the snow on the other side of the comm.

"Huh? Ms. Risya, are you running right now?"

"Yup, that's right. With Mismis!" Risya's voice was still upbeat. **"You two did a good job. You can leave the rest to us now. We've got all the pieces laid out for a big win!"**

"What? Are you making more deliveries?"

"That's right. The last spot is perfect. It's—"

Just then, Nameless and Mei, who had been listening in, breathed in sharply.

"You don't mean…"

"Risya, are you trying to get—"

The two seemed to understand her plan.

The place that got the highest volume of New Year's missives wasn't any high-rise condo. No, the most important location was actually…

"Ahh-ha-ha-ha! Aw, my plan is perfect!"

On Main Street, Risya's voice echoed all around the quiet buildings covered in snow.

"R-Risya, you're being too loud!"

"It's fine, Mismis. We've basically won. This is checkmate. We'd come out on top even if an elementary schooler was making this delivery."

Mismis was carrying a giant backpack stuffed with cards as she ran beside Risya, who had on a nearly identical backpack.

"But we don't have any time left!"

"It's still four thirty. We can get there in five."

There was a difference of a few thousand between their numbers and Division V's. Since the competition lasted until five in the morning, they had thirty more minutes left. That wasn't a number the two of them could make up for by themselves, but…

"There's a way to turn the tables on them!"

To do that, Mismis and Risya were trekking to a destination located deep within the capital.

"We've still got the Lord's office!"

That was where the Lord lived. No citizen of the Empire was unaware of that fact. That was even the location of the conference room where they had first been informed of the competition.

"The citizens are all very loyal, so they send His Excellency letters every single year to celebrate the New Year. That's easily several tens of thousands!" Risya explained.

"I see! So that's why we headed off separately…"

"Now you get it. We have the cards for His Excellency in our backpacks. We just need to bring them to the reception desk—"

With just a few thousand more cards, Risya's team would win. They'd make a huge comeback. She'd actually sent Iska and Jhin over to the condo building to distract Nameless and Mei.

"I had Isk and Jhinjhin act as decoys so we could get to the Lord's office and get a bunch of deliveries all at once. I saw all this coming! Ah, I am a true genius. What really counts in the end is having brains! I'm nothing like those two divisions—all they do is fulfill the mission they're given!"

"Risya, you sure seem excited…"

"Hee-hee. Just think of it as a sign that I've got confidence to spare."

They caught sight of the giant building, which was illuminated with security lights.

"This is way easier than doing little deliveries to individuals around the capital. Compared to those meat brains—"

"Risya, over there!"

"What?"

Mismis pointed behind them at the path they had just ran down. Against the backdrop of the city, two figures suddenly leaped out of the snow.

"I found you, Risya!"

"You've signed your own death warrant. You're gloating when you haven't even won yet."

"Ugh! Ms. Mei! And Nameless!"

It was the leaders of the two divisions Risya was up against. They were running over so fast that they were practically bulldozing through the snow.

Saint Disciples were the strongest forces in the Empire, so a little snow was no obstacle when they were really motivated.

"Oh no! They figured it out?!"

"See, Risya?! That's why I was trying to point out that you were too confident."

"We have to run, Mismis!"

"I already am!"

The two women increased their pace, but they were up against two other members of the armed forces. The distance between them was rapidly closing.

"Risya, I—I can't anymore. They're going to catch up!"

"No, Mismis. You can't give up yet."

"What?"

"Oops! I slipped!"

Risya flipped around. She roundhouse-kicked a snow-covered trash can, which rolled along the ground, picking up more snow and turning into a sort of avalanche that was headed right for Mei.

"Whoa?!" Mei quickly dodged it. Though she'd managed to avoid the trash can, she had gotten stuck in the snow.

"Why you little…!"

"Ah-ha-ha. Whoopsies!" Risya yelled.

"Oh, is that how you want to play it…? Fine!"

Mei kicked the trash can, too. But instead of aiming for Risya, she sent it hurtling beside her at Nameless.

"Mei, how dare you."

"Well, you just kept running while I was dealing with the trash! I'm not going to be the only one suffering indignity here!"

The two glared at each other. But that had been Risya's plan, too.

"Okay, let's keep it going, Mismis. While those two idiots are still fighting!"

"Who are you calling an idiot…?" Nameless scoffed. *"I'd like to see you try making it."*

"Wh-what is this?! Risya, look at that!" Mismis stopped in her tracks. She pointed ahead at the Lord's office, which seemed to be surrounded by glittering threads. "Are those wires?!"

"Risya, I knew you would go after the Lord's office," Nameless declared. *"Those touch-sensitive wires are rigged with explosives. To put it plainly, if you touch a wire, you explode."*

"Guh?!" Risya stopped in her tracks.

Layers of glittering wires were set up all around the gate to the Lord's office.

"R-Risya, we can't get in now!"

"......Yes. I miscalculated!" Risya bit her lip in frustration. "I didn't expect you to use the same trap, Nameless..."

"What?" Nameless seemed slightly distressed. *"You didn't, did you, Risya?"*

"Mismis, careful!" Risya pointed at the wires blocking their path. "This whole place is rigged with explosive wires. Both Nameless and I set the same traps!"

"Why do you both think alike only when it comes to this?!"

"Well...," Mei muttered to herself then. "Guess that makes three of us."

"Excuse me?"

"What?"

"What did you just say, Mei?" Nameless asked.

"I set some up, too. Those wire bombs." Mei awkwardly scratched the back of her head. "I *was* thinking that the front of the Lord's office looked weird. It seemed like way too many wires for what I'd set up. But if all three of us did the same thing, then the math checks out."

"__________"

"..."

The Saint Disciples fell silent. All three of them had unexpectedly set up wire traps at the Lord's office.

"Huh? But this is bad. If we trip even one wire, it'll cause a chain reaction of explosions. Mismis, be carefu—"

Bip.

Before Risya's very eyes...

"Oh..."

...Mismis bumped her toe against a wire.

It had been covered in snow.

"Mismis!"

"This isn't my fault, okay?!"

Bip, bip, bipbip.

A series of electronic tones followed. The instant after this chorus of electronic beeps went off, every last wire exploded in a chain reaction.

Three people's worth of explosives went off right in front of the Lord's office.

3

Two hours later.

The first rays of sun were peaking over the horizon.

"Hwaaah."

In the middle of the Lord's office, a silver beastperson stifled a small yawn. The beast's entire body was covered in a thick coat of fur like a fox's, but they seemed oddly welcoming—and resembled a cross between a girl and a cat.

This beast was the leader of the Empire, Lord Yunmelngen.

"So Imperial soldiers are supposed to protect the Empire. Isn't that right?"

"......Yes."

"I can't believe that Saint Disciples—the people who should be serving as role models for the other soldiers—set up an explosion in front of my office."

"...I'm very sorry."

"I thought the Founder had woken up at first."

"I'm so sorry for all the trouble we caused you."

BOO

The Lord sat cross-legged. Risya stood at attention in front of them, nursing the burns on her face. She was currently being scolded.

"We even had to use the anti-fire shutters we prepped for the Founder. Thanks to that, damage was kept to a minimum."

"If there wasn't much damage, then did you really need to lecture me for hours?"

"Did you say something?"

"No, nothing at all!"

After they had put out the fire from the gigantic explosion, Risya rang in the new year with a two-hour scolding session from the Lord.

Secret

Or the Prediction the World Doesn't Know Of

New Story

Our Last CRUSADE OR THE RISE OF A New World

Secret File

1

The area known as the Imperial capital. A century ago, this place had been turned into a sea of flames by the Founder Nebulis. It had been reborn like a phoenix into a city of steel.

This is a story from some years ago at a training organization located on the outskirts of the Imperial capital called the Bird's Nest.

2

Six in the morning.

Light slowly filtered through the gaps between the buildings of the Imperial capital as the sun rose.

Iska kept calling the name of his friend. "Gauch? Hey, Gauch, it's your turn to prep breakfast today. If you don't hurry, you'll get in trouble with our teacher again."

He walked down the old hallway.

Once he'd gotten to the room of his friend, who was boarding in the training facility with him, he knocked on the door.

"C'mon, Gauch, you can't sleep forever. If you don't hurry and wake up, Jhin and I will get in trouble, too. Hey…I'm opening the door."

He'd finally grown impatient.

"C'mon, Gauch… Gauch? ……"

The room was empty. All he found was a shabby desk and bed, and a wide-open window. He saw no sign of his friend, who had been living here until just yesterday.

Iska was struck speechless.

"He snuck out," a voice came from behind Iska, who was standing there in a daze.

A silver-haired boy leaned against the wall and murmured with a sigh, "Probably from that window he left open. He didn't leave any of his stuff behind, so I'm 99 percent sure. I thought I heard a lotta noise coming from his room yesterday."

"Jhin, why didn't you stop him?!"

"What was I supposed to do if I did?"

"Guh."

He had no idea how to respond to Jhin's retort. Though he sounded cold, he was actually the opposite. Jhin hadn't stopped Gauch because he cared for him.

Iska understood that. He really did. That was why all he could do was awkwardly smile.

"Looks like we've got more room again for the two of us."

"We've basically got the whole place to ourselves. We're the only ones left."

"And our teacher?" Iska said.

"He's the one who gives the lashings," Jhin replied. "I was talking about us just now, the ones on the receiving end."

"Yeah, I guess."

That was what the Bird's Nest was. This was a facility made so that Crossweil, the Black Steel Gladiator, could find his successor following his departure from the Saint Disciples.

He would wander wherever he pleased all over the Empire, scouting possible candidates from among the young boys he found. He had initially assembled several hundred candidates, like how a bird would gather hundreds of branches to make a nest.

The former strongest person in the Empire had gathered young talent from all over.

"What'll we do about breakfast? Me? Or you this time?"

Iska thought for a while, then shrugged. "Let's do it together, I guess."

They were the only two who had made it through Crossweil's brutal training, Jhin and Iska.

"I'll toast up the bread so, Jhin, you—"

"Morning!" a cheerful girl's voice called to them from the entrance. Then they heard the sounds of footsteps pattering through the hall.

"Good morning to my big bros!"

A girl, who was most likely twelve or thirteen, made her way to them. Her eyes were innocent, and her long red ponytail complemented her bubbly personality.

"Morning, Nene. What're you doing here today?"

"Hee-hee. I brought you something special." She'd hauled in a suitcase that was much too large for a young girl. "You said earlier that the TV was broken, right, Iska?"

"Oh, yeah, it is. Our teacher tried to fix it, but instead he—"

"I'll build a TV for you."

"Build one?!"

"That's right. I got the parts for cheap at a junkyard." Nene opened the suitcase. A monitor that was just big enough to fill their arms was sitting inside it.

"You're making this, Nene?"

"It's an international TV. It'll pick up any signal, no matter how weak it is. You'll even be able to watch Sovereignty programs."

"How'd you manage that?!" Iska cried out.

Then they heard the creak of the floor.

"Jhin."

"Hm? Master?"

Jhin turned around when he heard his whispered name.

A man dressed in black stood there. He was the Black Steel Gladiator, Crossweil Nes Lebeaxgate. The black-haired man was slender and muscular. He was wearing a long coat even though he was indoors.

"I need to discuss something with you. Come to my room," Crossweil whispered in a voice so low that Iska and Nene couldn't hear.

Jhin reluctantly followed his teacher.

Once Jhin and his teacher had settled into another room, Crossweil stood with his back to the morning sun.

"It's just you and Iska left now. You're the only two who made it without giving up."

His voice seemed unusually firm.

The man continued, "I found you at an Imperial forge, and

Iska in the corner of a park playing with a branch. You just never know. I didn't think Iska, the one with the lowest prospects, would stick it out this long."

"I think she has pretty good chances, too," Jhin said.

"'She'?"

"I mean Nene."

They heard excited talking coming from the hallway. Few people visited the Bird's Nest, but Nene was the exception.

"She's athletic enough to keep up with me and Iska when we go on our runs. And her engineering skills are inspiring, even though I'm not sure where they came from. Why not take Nene as an apprentice to replace Gauch?"

"I can't."

"Why not?"

"I don't have fond memories of women. My older sister once tried to kill me when she was really angry."

"...You have a sister?"

Crossweil had never brought up his family before. He only mentioned something about himself once a year or so.

"It's all in the past. Anyway, I'll give you a serious answer for once. Nene is exceptional. Even I can't find a flaw about her."

"Then you won't take her on because she's a girl?"

"She's too smart."

Uncharacteristically, the most socially awkward person in the Empire gave Jhin a forced smile.

"My successor has to be someone who's stupid. Someone who's smart will instinctively know whether something is possible or impossible, right? So Nene isn't cut out for this."

"Then I'm not, either?"

"That's right."

His master's words were merciless. After training up until now at this facility, right at the last minute, Jhin had been branded a candidate with zero prospects.

"Then why am I still here? If I'm not cut out for it, then you should've shooed me away already."

"Because I need you."

"?"

"I'm entrusting the astral swords to Iska, but I need you to stick behind him."

"Behind him?" Jhin just tilted his head quizzically. What did that even mean? Normally, wouldn't the stock phrase be to "stick beside" him?

"What's that supposed to mean?"

"I mean keep an eye on that idiot so he doesn't do anything reckless." Crossweil let out a sigh. "That idiot...Iska doesn't know when to quit—and I mean that in both a good and a bad way. If someone doesn't keep an eye on him, he'll pick a fight with the Imperial forces and end up in prison."

"C'mon, you're exaggerating."

"It's your job to stop him. So you'll be a sniper. Stick to the very back of the unit and keep an eye on Iska."

Jhin didn't reply.

"Right," Crossweil said. "Nene could even be part of that unit."

The man in black turned around. He stared into the blinding light that had once lit his back.

"Let Iska kick up a fuss, and you and Nene support him from behind. That's not too bad, balance-wise. And..."

"And?"

"You'll need a boss—an adult—to keep you coordinated. The three of you will still be too immature, even a few years from now."

The strongest Imperial swordsman suddenly let out a sigh. "Do you understand?"

"You're entrusting the astral swords to Iska. But Iska would go rogue if he were left alone, so you want me to babysit him. And you figure Nene might as well join us. But the three of us alone won't cut it, so we need some sorta leader."

"That's perfect."

That was the closest thing to praise that would come from his incredibly taciturn master.

"You've got the brains that Iska doesn't. Make sure to take care of that head of yours."

"Sure..."

They left it at that, and Jhin headed outside of his master's room.

"An Imperial unit, huh...?"

Him. Iska. Nene.

They'd need one more person who'd be able to act as their commander.

"Wait... He didn't call me in there because he wants me to find a boss?" Jhin murmured to himself as he walked down the hall.

3

And now...

"I see. So that's what your teacher or whatever is like."

"In the end, I never found anyone we could really call an adult. Instead, I wound up with a commander who looks and acts like a little kid."

They were in a park in the Imperial capital.

Jhin and Sisbell were sitting together on a bench.

"Hey, Jhin?!" Commander Mismis was heading toward them at a ferocious clip.

She was petite and had a baby face; she seemed like a far cry from the "boss" their master had intended them to have.

"We need to save Miss Rin and meet with the Lord… Wait, what are you talking about at a time like this?!"

"About Iska and my master. What else am I supposed to do? Sisbell insisted on hearing more about him."

"You were definitely saying something mean about me!"

"No, I was praising you," Jhin shot back, and stood from the bench.

A large road led out of the park. Nene and Saint Disciple Risya were waiting for them there.

"The master was absolutely right about Iska picking a fight with the Imperial forces and winding up in prison. I never thought he'd actually do it."

"? What's going on?" Iska stared in disbelief at them.

There had been the witch jailbreak incident. A year ago, the foolhardy successor they were just talking about had actually gone through with a plan without telling anyone. As a result, he had been incarcerated for treason. Everything had played out exactly as their teacher had predicted.

"Iska."

"What?" Iska turned around as his name was called.

"We're going to see the Lord now," Jhin said. "But Rin's also held up there."

"…Yeah."

"Don't go on a rampage unless I'm there to keep an eye on you."

"Why are you assuming that I'd go on a rampage?!"

"I'm saying it just in case. If somebody doesn't tell you that, you dive headfirst without thinking," Jhin told him matter-of-factly.

He looked up at the Lord's office, which was illuminated ahead on the main road.

Afterword

Thank you for picking up the second volume of *Our Last Crusade or the Rise of a New World* (*Last Crusade*)'s short stories!

How did you like it?

This special volume contains some of the short stories serialized in the bimonthly *Dragon Magazine*!

I really had trouble figuring out which stories to include in this one, too… (Ha-ha.)

Allow me to introduce the stories themselves right away and to talk about the "Secret Files" that show anecdotal glimpses into Iska's everyday life and Alice's palace life.

◇ File 01 "Our Last Crusade or the Artist of Fire" (September 2018)

The living treasure, Master Daiban, makes his first appearance.

Of the characters who show up in the short stories, he has a particularly unique spark. He's a living legend in the art world and has a passionate international fan base, which includes art lovers like Iska and Alice…but that's not all there is to him.

Master Daiban actually has a major role in the main story.

When this short story was published, Lord Yunmelngen's form was still a secret in the main story. Masterpiece No. 9 is actually the first depiction of the Lord in their true form as a beastperson.

Then there's Daiban's opera masterwork, *Our Last Crusade or the Rise of a New World Love Sonata.*

Daiban was asked to write the song for a young man three decades ago, and you may recognize that as a significant number from the main story.

That's right.

Thirty years ago, right before he ended up in prison, a certain sorcerer commissioned Daiban to write a song that would convey his feelings to someone who didn't understand how he felt about her.

(Please take a peek at Volume 6 if you'd like to know more.)

The unfinished magnum opus will be completed soon…

But that's for another time…

◇ File 2 "Our Last Crusade or the Spy Mission Training" (March 2019)

This is when Commander Pilie gets her revenge (kind of).

Just like Master Daiban, P is a character just for the short stories.

If I say that this is a regular day for her in the Imperial forces… that might be misleading. Commander Pilie is actually an excellent soldier. But whenever she's up against Mismis, she rapidly loses all common sense and her faculties for judgment…

* * *

File 3 "Our Last Crusade or the Turbulent Halloween Party" (January 2019)

In this story, Master Daiban gets his second bombastic introduction.

Iska and Alice almost cross paths, Rin puts in a big effort, and Commander Mismis and Nene get up to some fun. It's my favorite of these stories.

In this tale, it's also revealed that Master Daiban has had a meeting with Elletear from the Lou family.

There are other Easter eggs where the short stories and main work intersect (not just when it comes to Master Daiban). I hope that you'll find them!

◇ File 04 "Our Last Crusade or the Undefeatable Big Sister" (July 2020)

This story was written in celebration of *Last Crusade* being on the cover of *Dragon Magazine* for the first time!

Since I'd been writing only for Fantasia Bunko, this was my first time having something on the cover of a *Dragon Magazine* issue.

Since it was a special issue I was commemorating, I wanted to write something special, too.

So I put the spotlight on the three sisters, which hadn't happened since the sixth volume.

This was all about how Elletear is the strongest big sister ever. It's also unusual to see Alice and Sisbell joining forces. (Ha-ha.)

◇ File XX "The Strongest Combatants Serving the Lord" (New story)

This ended up becoming a pretty long new story about the Saint Disciples.

In addition to Risya, even Nameless and Mei join in.

Nameless showed up in the anime, and it seems like his battle with Alice was well-received not only in Japan, but also internationally!

And because of the response to the anime, I had Nameless appear in this competition, too.

Mei hasn't shown up in the anime, but some people might remember her from the seventh volume when she fought against Kissing, the Thorn Witch.

My concept for this story was to portray a merciless battle among the three Saint Disciples.

◇ Secret "Or the Prediction the World Doesn't Know Of" (New story)

This story closes off the Secret Files for this volume.

I've revealed some of Iska's conversations with Crossweil, but this one focuses on a conversation with Jhin.

This is where it's shown what role Jhin is given as a young man and how the group (including Nene) needed an adult to act as a "boss."

Also, this epilogue is the story that occurs the most recently, as far as chronological order goes.

It's right between Volumes 10 and 11, so you can wonder how this epilogue connects with the main story.

I hope that you enjoy it!

▼The *Last Crusade* TV anime is airing.

The anime should be reaching its climax by the time this volume of short stories comes out.

How have you liked it so far? I'm excited every time I watch the anime, and fortunately, many people in Japan and around the world are enjoying it, too.

Three months of airing really go by quickly!

Well then…

With the anime comes BluRays and DVD releases. These will be available soon.

BluRay/DVD Vol. 1: January 27, 2021 (Eps. 1–4)

BluRay/DVD Vol. 2: February 24, 2021 (Eps. 5–8)

BluRay/DVD Vol. 3: March 24, 2021 (Ep. 9–12)

There are a lot of extras that are available with the purchases, but I'd like to talk about the extra stories I wrote specifically.

▼Anime Special Novel

I think some of you may already know this…

Last Crusade is my first work that was turned into an anime. From the script meetings to the recording sessions, and the actual broadcast of the anime, there's so much I'll remember, but having *Last Crusade* turned into BluRays and DVDs is like a dream come true.

And that's why I'd like to make sure to give the best new story I can to the people who liked the anime and bought the BluRays and DVDs,

So, at the time, I pondered about what that new story would be.

Since I was writing about Iska and Alice in the main story and the short stories, I thought I'd write about the characters living in the background of *Last Crusade*'s world—in other words, the heroes and heroines behind the scenes.

This is only available with the anime BluRay and DVDs.

These are the stories of the former main characters and former heroines.

* * *

▼Anime BluRay/DVD commemoration, special novel

BluRay/DVD Vol. 1: Forbidden Chapter—The Founder

In the third episode of the anime, Iska and Alice had their battle with the Founder Nebulis.

This story is about that battle from the Founder's point of view.

I think from Iska and Alice's perspective, she seemed like a villain who indiscriminately attacked Rin and the neutral city.

But what did the Founder think?

What was she thinking as she fought Iska and Alice?

Her mind was on something completely different, and this is a story about her perspective as a last boss character.

This is about the wish that the Founder has deep inside that the anime and the first volume couldn't cover.

I hope that once you get the novel, you'll take a look at it.

BluRay/DVD Vol. 2: Forbidden Chapter—The Sorcerer

This is the story of Salinger.

As those reading the novels might know, this sorcerer should have previously been a main character, but he was brought down by a plot.

This is about what Salinger was thinking in the anime and the third volume when he faced Iska and Rin.

His story is also related to the grand chorus, *Our Last Crusade or the Rise of a New World Love Sonata*. I also put a lot of effort into writing this one.

BluRay/DVD vol. 3: Prohibited Chapter—The Astral Powers and the Black Steel

Since the last episode of the anime hasn't aired yet, I'm just revealing the title for this one. Maybe you've already guessed what this might be about?

I'll give more details on my X account on a future date!

Well then…

The novels and the anime are getting closer to their climaxes, and I'd like to talk a bit more about the future.

I have another new book that I've been writing alongside *Last Crusade*.

Please allow me to introduce my newest story!

A battle of the brains between humans and gods.

The supreme gods have created the ultimate challenge: the divine games. In all of recorded history, no one has had a winning streak. The competition against the all-powerful gods starts here.

▼ *Gods' Games We Play* is coming out January 25th (Monday) from MF Bunko J.

Humanity must win ten games of wits against the gods to be victorious.

In this tale, a young man takes up an impossible challenge.

We actually plan to air a commercial for it during the twelfth episode of *Last Crusade*'s anime.

Sora Amamiya will be doing the commercial!

That's right. Amamiya, who also voices Alice, will be doing the voice for the commercial for my new work. I hope that you watch it!

So…

I've started another story in addition to *Last Crusade.*

I'll work as hard as I can so you can enjoy it, and I'll be so happy if you pick it up at a bookstore!

Looks like the afterword is nearing its end, too.

(I'm going to thank everyone involved in the anime after it finishes airing…)

First, to Ao Nekonabe, who drew another first-rate cover! Thank you very much! Sisbell looks so cute in her personal clothes!

To my editors O and S, I know you're very busy with the novels and the anime. Thank you so much for everything.

The anime is also reaching its climax, but I wouldn't have been able to get here without you two.

I'll be so happy if you'll help me for just a little longer!

Next is *Last Crusade*, Vol. 11.

A tale of the swordsman Iska and the witch princess Alice.

And also a story about siblings who go by the name of Nebulis.

Please look forward to reading this account of heroes and heroines past, revealed through Sisbell's power of Illumination.

Well, see you next year.

Gods' Games We Play comes out on January 25th from MF Bunko J.

Last Crusade, Vol. 11 will be out in the spring.

I hope that you'll also see the final episode of the anime.

On an unusually warm winter's day,

Kei Sazane